GRACE

Books by Shelley Shepard Gray

The Sisters of the Heart Series

HIDDEN
WANTED
FORGIVEN
GRACE

The Seasons of Sugarcreek Series

WINTER'S AWAKENING
SPRING'S RENEWAL
AUTUMN'S PROMISE

GRACE

A Christmas Sisters *of the* Heart Novel

SHELLEY SHEPARD GRAY

AVON

INSPIRE

An Imprint of HarperCollins*Publishers*

GRACE. Copyright © 2010 by Shelley Shepard Gray. All rights reserved. Printed in the United States of America. No part of this book may be used or reproduced in any manner whatsoever without written permission except in the case of brief quotations embodied in critical articles and reviews. For information address HarperCollins Publishers, 10 East 53rd Street, New York, NY 10022.

HarperCollins books may be purchased for educational, business, or sales promotional use. For information please write: Special Markets Department, HarperCollins Publishers, 10 East 53rd Street, New York, NY 10022.

FIRST AVON PAPERBACK EDITION PUBLISHED 2010.

Designed by Diahann Sturge

Library of Congress Cataloging-in-Publication Data
    Gray, Shelley Shepard.
      Grace : a Christmas sisters of the heart novel / Shelley Shepard Gray. — 1st
    Avon pbk. ed.
          p.   cm. — (Sisters of the heart)
      ISBN 978-0-06-199096-0 (pbk.)
      1. Christmas stories.   I. Title.
    PS3607.R3966G73 2010
    813'.6—dc22   2010027297

10 11 12 13 14   OV/RRD   10 9 8 7 6 5 4 3 2 1

To Tom.
Wherever you are, it is home.

The author is grateful for being allowed
to reprint recipes from *Our Family's Favorite Recipes*

The Shrock's Homestead
9943 Copperhead Rd. N.W.
Sugarcreek, OH 44681

God's mercy is great, and he loved us very much. Though we were spiritually dead because of the things we did against God, he gave us new life with Christ. You have been saved by God's grace.

—Ephesians 2:4–5

Will you rejoice in the birth of the King? Or just in the things Christmas will bring?

—Amish proverb

GRACE

Chapter 1

December 20, 8:00 A.M.

"Anna!" The Christmas bells hanging on the wooden door of Katie Lundy's childhood home, the Brenneman Bed and Breakfast, tinkled as she entered. Her gaze drifted to a pair of candles adorned with red ribbons on the front table, and a familiar warmth settled over her. "Anna? Are you here?" she again called out.

Before she had completely shut the heavy door, her parents started fussing.

"Katie, whyever are you creating such a ruckus in the house?" Her mother's form suddenly appeared in the doorway leading to the kitchen. Wiping her hands on her apron, she chided, "You could have woken up all of our guests."

From the other side of the foyer, her father came into sight. "Yes, Katie, that yelling would be a problem . . . if we did have a houseful, which we do not, thankfully." As he looked her over, his frown contrasted with the twinkle in his eyes. "But you are loud enough to wake the dead, child."

No matter how old she got, receiving criticism from her parents never failed to make her cheeks bloom like roses in July. "I'm sorry." Making sure to keep her voice down, she craned her neck to look beyond her mother into the cozy kitchen. "I'm looking for Anna. Is she here?"

"I am," Anna announced from the landing at the top of the stairs. Looking down at Katie from the well-polished banister, her best friend and sister-in-law smirked. "I think someone is excited to go shopping today."

There was no reason to lie. She *was* eager about their planned outing for the day. "I can't help it. It's been a long time since we've played hooky."

Her mother grinned. "If you're this wound up about a shopping trip, I'm thinking you should plan more outings."

"It's only because they are so rare that I'm excited. If it was a usual occurrence, it wouldn't matter so much." As Anna walked down the steps, Katie continued. "Jonathan got an unexpected day off at the lumberyard, so he's with the girls and Eli."

Her mother clucked. "You should have brought the *boppli* here. I would have happily taken care of him."

"Jonathan didn't mind watching the baby. Besides, I wasn't sure if you had houseguests."

"It's December twentieth. Of course we don't have houseguests," her mother said. "All I'm doing is getting the house readied for our family holiday."

Though they never formally closed the inn for the celebration of the Lord's birth, Katie couldn't remember when they'd ever hosted guests at the inn during this time.

Once the calendar marked December fifteenth, visitors suddenly stopped arriving. Their absence allowed the large, rambling house to become a home once again.

This year, in honor of young Eli's birth and Anna and Henry's marriage, everyone decided to spend a whole week together: Katie and her family; Anna and Henry; Rebekeh and her family; and this year, at Anna's and Katie's request, Winnie—Jonathan's sister—and Winnie's husband Samuel were going to stay the week of Christmas as well.

Yes, the house was going to be mighty full, but joyous and merry, too. It would be the perfect time for Katie to take a breath and rejuvenate. Lately, she'd been so tired, it was all she could do to keep her eyes open at night. Once or twice, she'd even fallen asleep during Eli's nap.

Jonathan thought she was doing too much, and she probably was. She had many responsibilities now, with a home, a three-month-old baby, and two busy stepdaughters.

But all of it was a joy. And nothing that couldn't be made better with a little bit of comfort from her parents.

Speaking again, her mother worried her bottom lip. "I went shopping yesterday, but I feel sure I didn't buy enough flour and sugar."

"Just give me a list, Mamm," Katie said. "I'll pick up

whatever I can." Katie was just about to motion for Anna to hurry and put on her boots and cloak when Henry walked down the stairs waving a sheet of paper.

"I'm afraid our plans are about to change," he murmured.

When he stopped by his bride's side, Anna pulled the paper out of his hand. Moments later, she frowned. "Oh, no."

Katie strode closer, her mother right behind her. "What on earth is wrong?" she asked. "You both look like you've seen a ghost."

"This is a mailed-in reservation," Anna murmured.

"So? What's special about that? We get them all the time."

Henry showed them the envelope he still held in his hands. "Our zip code was either written wrong or the mail carrier couldn't read it. So, from the postdate, it looks like it's been on a trip around Ohio."

Katie tapped her foot. "And? Come on, Henry. I want to go look at fabric."

"Well, the fact of the matter is, Mr. Levi Bender is planning to arrive here today"—he pointed to a sentence at the bottom of the page—"and we were supposed to have contacted him if we were full up by the eighteenth."

Katie's mother leaned her hand on the banister with a sigh. "And here it is December twentieth. How long will he stay, Henry?"

"Through the holiday," he said grimly. "He says here until December twenty-eighth."

Although she knew it wasn't a Christian response, Katie felt a swarm of irritation buzz through her as all her plans began to evaporate. She'd been looking forward to only being surrounded by family for the next week or so. It had been such a crazy year and a half, with Anna and her brother marrying, she marrying Jonathan . . . his barn burning down, Winnie in the hospital.

And Eli being born in October. All Katie wanted to do was enjoy peace and quiet and her family. She didn't want to have to cook and clean for a guest. She didn't want to have to keep reminding her girls to keep their voices down, either.

"This man is going to ruin our Christmas! Can't we turn him away?"

Her father glared. "Of course not."

Her mother walked to her *daed*'s side. "Well, we're just going to have to be grateful for a Christmas guest. That's all there is to it."

"But now how are we all going to stay here together?"

"One man's arrival won't change things." A line appeared between her mother's brows. "Not too much, anyway."

Katie reached for Anna's hand. "Anna, let's get going now, then. With a guest arriving, chances are *gut* that we won't have another chance to get away."

With a look of regret, Anna shook her head. "I'm sorry, Katie, but I won't be able to go. If we have a guest coming, I'll need to prepare a room."

With a sense of dismay, Katie felt all her anticipated plans fall to the wayside. "But—"

Anna turned away from her. "Irene, which room would you like to put him in?"

"In the room up at the top of the stairs, I suppose. It's our best room."

She was talking about the attic room, of course. The room Katie had planned to occupy with Jonathan. It was lovely, and claimed its own private bathroom—something that Katie had been looking forward to since she still woke up often with Eli.

As everyone looked upstairs rather mournfully, her mother sighed. "I have to say that having a guest here for Christmas has put me in a dither. What in the world are we going to do with Mr. Levi Bender here for the next eight days?"

One by one, everyone scattered. Soon, only Katie stood alone in the foyer. A strong sense of loss filled her. And though she knew it was not their guest's fault, she couldn't help but feel resentful. No matter how pleasant the man was, his presence was going to spoil their relaxed holiday plans. "Levi Bender, how in the world are we going to be able to get rid of you?" she murmured . . . just before she finally unhooked her cloak and joined her mother in the kitchen.

December 20, 2:00 P.M.

It had taken him all day to get there. First, Levi had had to rise with the roosters at dawn and tend to his small menagerie of animals. Then, after checking and double-checking that all was in order for the two teenaged boys who would be staying at his home for the week, he'd waited for the *Englischer* to pick him up and drive him to the bus station in Columbus.

Because snow was still falling, the bus was running an hour late. Levi had sat in his chair and sipped a too-expensive coffee out of a Styrofoam cup that a vendor had been selling right there in the lobby. He'd kept to himself and tried not to notice the looks of interest passing his way. Those same looks that he always felt whenever he was in the outside world.

After claiming a seat on the bus, he'd ridden for two hours, switched buses, and then rode for another hour and a half to Peebles. Now he was in an *Englischer*'s car again. On his way to the Brenneman Bed and Breakfast.

"So, have you been to this area before?"

"No."

"Oh. You got family out here?"

In spite of the generic question, Levi felt a shudder rustle through him. "No," he said again, this time with more force.

In the rearview mirror, the taxi driver raised his eyebrows. "Sorry, buddy. Didn't know that was a sore subject." His tone and the slight inflection at the end of his reply led Levi to believe that the driver was waiting for more explanation.

Levi merely looked out the window. In his experience, that was how most *Englischers* were—too nosy about things that didn't concern them at all.

Because he certainly wasn't going to tell anyone why he'd left his community to travel by himself for Christmas. Why he'd rather stay in the company of strangers than in the midst of people who'd known him all of his life. Why he was willing to sleep in a small guest room with only a bathroom down the hall than spend another night in his own bed—in a house that he and Rosanna had designed and help build.

Rosanna!

Even just thinking her name brought a fresh wave of sorrow, like a toothache he couldn't help but probe, bringing more pain to the surface. Since he was already hurting, Levi pushed himself to recall another person who had once meant so much to him . . . Ruth.

As the taxi traveled the winding roads toward the inn, Levi closed his eyes and let the agony fill his body for one last time before he pretended that the two most important women in his life had never existed.

Of course, that was the crux of it all . . . wasn't it? Rosanna and Ruth weren't around, and they never would be again. Ever.

Because he'd killed them.

December 20, 3:30 P.M.

"Miss? Do you need any help, miss?" the *Englischer* asked with a concerned expression. "You look like you've kind of got your hands full there."

Melody still got spooked talking with strange men. But as the moment passed between them, and he kept rudely staring at her, awaiting a response, she shook her head. "No." Hurt flashed into his eyes. "I mean, *Dank*—Thank you. But no, I'm fine."

After treating her to another long look of doubt at the

quilt bag on her lap and the worn suitcase under her feet, he shrugged and walked away.

"Don't you mind the driver, miss," said an elderly lady sitting across the aisle from her on the bus. "I've ridden with Graham before and he's a worrier. Always has been. And, well, pardon my sayin' so, but you do look like you're about to deliver at any moment."

Shamed, Melody turned to the window and hugged her quilt bag more tightly.

It had been a long journey to Cincinnati, Ohio, from Sonora, Kentucky. It had taken almost as long for her to find the correct bus to take her to Adams County. Now she was in a hired van to the Brenneman Bed and Breakfast to spend the next week, if she was lucky.

Her employer, Mrs. Sheridan had given her some money and a gift certificate when Melody had come to work in the coffee shop looking even worse than usual. "I really think you need to take some time off, dear."

"I'm fine," she'd murmured, mainly because she had no choice. This was her job.

As if Mrs. Sheridan had read her mind, she murmured, "No, dear, I don't think you are. Hold on a moment, I'll be right back."

Moments later, she handed Melody an envelope with a hundred dollar bill and a gift certificate inside. Melody had held it like it was on fire. "What is this?"

"It's an early Christmas gift. It's a certificate to the love-liest little inn north of Cincinnati. In Ohio."

"What would I do there?"

"Relax for a bit." Mrs. Sheridan's eyes softened as she recalled the place. "It's a real beauty of a place, I'll tell you that. The Brenneman Bed and Breakfast has a wide wooden porch in the front. It runs the whole front of the building. The house just shines, it does. It's all white-washed, and has shiny black shutters. In the spring, glorious flowers decorate every available inch of land around the house."

In spite of herself, Melody was mesmerized. "And in the winter?"

Her boss sighed. "In the winter, they decorate a bit with greenery. Nature provides holly bushes in the woods. Mrs. Brenneman clips some sprigs and places them in glass bowls. A few of the windows have candles and garlands. And they polish everything with the most heavenly scented orange oil. At night, when the snow is glistening outside and the rooms smell of hot spiced cider, wood from the fire, and orange oil . . . why I have to say there's nothing else in the world like it. You should go, dear."

For a moment, Melody, too, had been taken away. But even the thought of traveling by herself was disconcerting. As was the cost. "Thank you for the idea, but I'm afraid I can't accept such a gift. It's too much."

"Oh, it's not so much, really." All smiles, she explained, "Mr. Sheridan and I won this in a charity auction about six months ago. It's good for a week's stay."

In spite of her will not to, Melody found herself gripping the envelope. It took everything she had to weakly refuse one more time. "I couldn't."

"Yes, you could, Melody . . . if you dare. I think you need

some time off." Her voice lowered. "I know that things haven't been too good for you here. Sometimes, if you can't find a comforting place in your own hometown, it's time to venture somewhere else. Go there, Melody. Go to the Brennemans' and relax and learn to smile again. It will do you and the baby a world of good."

A world of good.

The kind words had rung in her ears the rest of the day. They were so different than everything else she was used to hearing. Most folks barely looked at her.

None directly spoke of her circumstances.

Yet, did she really imagine that people would speak of her, to her, frankly?

Plain and simply, she'd been raped by an *Englischer,* held apart by her family, and now was looking forward to forever being a symbol of foolish behavior in the eyes of everyone in her community. As in, *"Don't go walking alone like Melody did. Look what happened to her."*

As in, *"Look what happened to Melody. Now she's going to have to carry that burden for the rest of her life."*

As in, *"Melody, you've shamed us."*

Consequently, she'd retreated into herself. If others wouldn't have a care for her feelings, then she would.

That night, Melody had clumsily knelt by her bed and prayed. "What should I do?" she'd whispered.

Tightly, she'd closed her eyes. With bated breath, she'd strained to hear words of guidance. And then, like the gift that it was . . . she heard the Lord's voice.

Just as clearly as if he'd been standing at her shoulder. *Go, Melody. Go and learn to smile again.*

* * *

"Miss? You going to get up anytime soon?" the driver asked. "We're here."

She stood up with a start. Out of the window to her right was the Brenneman Bed and Breakfast, looking just as lovely as Mrs. Sheridan described.

"Oh! I'm . . . I'm sorry. I'll get my things and hurry out."

To her surprise, a woman sitting in front of her picked up the suitcase and carried it out of the van. The driver helped her down the step and took her payment easily, not even counting it before slipping it into his black wool coat.

"Merry Christmas," he murmured before closing his door and pulling out of the driveway.

Leaving her alone. Staring at the wide front steps. At the garland that was roped around the porch railing. Suddenly, everything seemed to be too much. The trip, the traveling, the stress. The cold. A wave of dizziness fell over her.

The front door opened. A pretty woman just about her age stepped out and stared. "May I help you?"

The world was tilting. Threatening to go black. "I'm Melody Gingerich."

Blue eyes narrowed. "And?"

"I . . . I came to stay for Christmas," she murmured. In a haze, she did her best to concentrate, but the woman's reaction was truly puzzling.

"You came to do what?" the girl asked, her voice sounding high pitched. Almost angry.

"I have a certificate."

"For what?"

As the girl's eyes continued to stare her down, Melody fumbled for a better explanation. But truly, all ideas fled her mind. She didn't know what to say. How to explain about everything she'd been through. Everything she'd done.

Then it didn't matter. Because her knees gave away, her world spun, and her suitcase fell to the ground with a thud.

Seconds later, she felt the cold icy snow cradle her cheek . . . as her world went black.

Chapter 2

December 20, 4:00 P.M.

The girl had fallen.

Heedless of the open door behind her, Katie ran out to the patch where the girl lay crumbled. A light amount of snow coated the ground, and moisture filtered through the heavy wool of her dress as she sank to her knees. "Miss?" she whispered. "Miss? Can you hear me?"

Unfortunately, no fluttering of eyelashes or gasp of surprise greeted her. Instead, the girl remained motionless, her gray dress and black apron in disarray around her ankles. Katie lifted the girl's hand and felt for a pulse along her wrist. She sighed in relief as a steady rhythm of blood coursed through the veins. "Oh, thank goodness," she breathed. For a moment, there, Katie had feared the worst.

Without regard for the damp ground, Katie sat down and resituated the girl's head. With an anxious heart, she slipped off her black traveling bonnet and carefully set her *kapp* to rights.

But still she lay there, quiet.

"What to do?" Katie murmured. Spying the white dishcloth that had fallen from her hand, Katie picked it up and folded it several times. Finally, she rested the girl's head on it. "At least your *kapp* might stay dry this way."

And still, the girl was unresponsive. "What could be wrong?" Katie murmured. Puzzled, she pressed her fingers to the girl's forehead. Perhaps she was feverish? No. Her skin was cool to the touch.

Though her brain told her the newcomer had simply passed out, Katie's heart began to pound. She'd never witnessed anyone being so unresponsive for so long.

And so she tried for a reaction yet again. "Miss? Can you hear me? Miss? Are you all right?"

Close up, she noticed that the girl's hair was a striking auburn, the color of a fox's coat in winter. The strands that had fallen out of the *kapp* and bonnet looked rich and lush against the her fair skin. By force of habit, she carefully smoothed back the hair, like she did with her stepdaughters.

That touch led to more methodical ones. Perhaps the girl had hit her head and was bleeding? As Katie examined the girl's scalp, looking for evidence of a serious injury, her own pulse raced. What were they going to do if this girl did indeed need emergency medical assistance?

Oh, she hoped not. They were far enough away from

the main roads that any ambulance would take at least ten or fifteen minutes. And that might be too late.

Oh, she needed this girl to rouse!

And once more Katie thought, perhaps it was all her fault she'd even fallen! No one needed to tell her how rude she'd been. Frantic now, she raised her voice. "Miss? Miss? Please answer!"

"Katie?" Anna called out from the door. "What's going on?"

In spite of the gravity of the situation, Katie took a moment to smile. No matter how "Amish" her friend Anna had become over the last two years, in many ways, she would always be English Anna. Some of her phrases and gestures were too imbedded to remove. "This girl— she fainted," Katie replied. "At least I think that is what has happened. I can't seem to rouse her."

"Is she injured?" Anna stepped forward, taking care to watch her footing on the slippery walkway. "Henry said he was going to salt this well, but maybe it's still icy? Perhaps she slipped and fell?"

"No, I don't think so. I . . . I was staring at her. Actually, Anna, I was *glaring* at her and asked what business she had here."

"And then?"

"And then she told me her name and then fainted."

"She's got to be cold. I'll go get a blanket."

"Hurry, Anna."

Before she turned away, Anna reached out and wrapped an arm around Katie, giving her comfort like she always did. For a moment Katie leaned close. "It will be okay," said Anna.

"I hope so."

As Anna turned and scampered back inside, Katie anxiously looked at the girl—and counted her blessings. Oh, she was so grateful to have a friend like Anna.

Moments later, Anna tucked a thick blanket around the girl. "I told Mamm to find Henry. We need to bring her inside. Do you happen to know what her name is?"

"Melody. I've already forgotten her last name, though." Shame burned her cheeks as she once again remembered how she'd greeted the girl. Now each rude gesture seemed to be magnified and terribly embarrassing. "Anna, I think maybe this is my fault. I wasn't very welcoming."

"No one faints from a poor welcome, Katie."

"I hope not. But I could have been nicer. No, that's not right. I *should* have been much nicer."

"Don't worry so. Regrets will only make you lose sleep, not solve the problem."

"That sounds Amish."

Anna smiled. "That's because I am, of course."

As they both looked at the girl—at Melody—with concern, Katie couldn't help but dwell on the fact that Anna hadn't attempted to soothe Katie's worries about her discourteousness. Was it because she'd noticed that Katie had been bad-mannered before?

"What are you two doing in the snow? Don'tcha think it's a bit cold out here for that?" Henry called out, striding forward from the barn. Before they could correct him, his eyes widened. "Ah."

"The girl is ill," Anna said. "And she's with child, too."

"We better take her inside," Henry said. "It's far too cold

to rest on the ground. I'll pick her up and carry her to the hearth room."

But just as Henry was about to slide an arm under the girl's back, Melody blinked, then peered at them.

At Henry. Immediately, her look of confusion slid into pure fright. "No!" she cried.

Henry immediately stepped backward. With both hands up as though he was at the mercy of a bank robber, he spoke slowly. "I'm sorry. I . . . I was just going to pick you up. Don't be afraid . . ."

The girl shook her head.

Katie could see her tremble. "Melody? You're at our inn. At the Brennemans'. A van dropped you off," she said as quietly and as clearly as she could. "Do you remember coming here?"

Slowly, their guest's eyes focused. She continued to stare at Henry. Finally, she nodded once.

Oh, thank goodness! "Do you remember seeing me?" she murmured.

When the girl still stared at them all confused, Anna took a turn. "It's okay," she soothed. "Don't try to get up. You fell. Do you remember that?"

She shook her head, darted a look Katie's way, then moaned again. "I'm sorry." Looking beyond Katie to Henry, awkwardly standing a few feet away, the girl swallowed hard. "I'm sorry," she said again. "I'm fine now."

"Are you hurt?" Katie asked.

"*Nee.*" She bit her lip, then shifted to a sitting position. "I guess all the traveling made me dizzy."

"And no wonder, you're going to have a baby!" Anna said as she scrambled to her feet. "That makes everything just a little harder, especially a long day of traveling. And here we are, keeping you out here on the sidewalk." Reaching out, she clutched the newcomer's arm. "Here, dear. Let us help you up."

Katie reached to help, too, instinctively knowing that the girl would shy away from Henry's touch. Grabbing the girl's other arm, they pulled her to her feet. Standing up, it was painfully obvious that Melody was extremely pregnant. "When is your baby due?"

"Three weeks."

"Three weeks? Then why in the world—"

Anna stilled the rest of Katie's question with a warning look. "Outside is no place to have a conversation. Let's get you inside, in front of a fire and warm you up. Would you care for some tea?"

"Yes," Melody said softly. *"Danke."*

They were up the steps and almost at the front door when a blue truck pulled up the long driveway. Seconds later, a man got out and grabbed a suitcase from out of the truck's back before it pulled away.

Though their arms were full with Melody, Katie didn't feel that she and Anna should turn their backs on the man. Henry had already gone into the barn, so there was no one else to greet him.

"I bet this is another guest," Katie mumbled. "Mr. Bender?" she called out. "Mr. Levi Bender?"

The man met her gaze with a fierce glare. "Yes, that is me."

Great. Their Christmas guest was a sourpuss. *"Wilkum!* Welcome to the Sugarcreek Inn," she said dutifully. "Please follow us in."

Now that Melody was steadier on her feet, Katie motioned for Anna to get the door. "Let's go inside now."

Alarmed, Melody pointed behind her. "I'm afraid my bag is still out there in the snow."

"I'll go out and fetch it just as soon as we get you inside," Anna said.

Mr. Bender must have heard her, because he abruptly turned away, marched back down the steps, stomped out to Melody's things and picked them up, too. "I've got them."

"Indeed you do," Anna said. "That is so very kind of you. *Danke.*"

Mr. Bender scowled in response.

Katie smiled weakly as they made their way into the house. And what a procession it was! Their sullen houseguest. Their pregnant stranger. And Anna, dear Anna, who was now acting more hospitable and Amish than she ever.

And herself. Katie. On the outside, she was doing her best to be welcoming; inside, she was filled with bitterness and resentment toward the newcomers. Without a doubt, these guests were odd. Strange. And they were ruining all the plans that had been made during the past month.

Once they entered the foyer, Anna pointed to the staircase. "Just set the bags down and follow us, Mr. Bender."

To Katie's amazement, he did just that, following Katie and Melody into the hearth room. Moments later, Melody was seated on the couch and her face seemed to gain some color.

Mr. Bender, in contrast, stood as far away from them as possible, arms crossed over his broad chest. His scowl had returned, especially every time he looked toward Melody.

Her mother's arrival broke the silence. "Ah, our visitor has arrived." She beamed. "Welcome. You are Mr. Bender, *jah*?"

"*Jah*. And *danke*."

"And we have another visitor, Mamm," Katie interjected quickly. "This is Melody."

As usual, her mother was nothing but generous and kind. "Welcome to our home, Melody. We hope you will enjoy your stay."

After asking who wanted coffee or tea, Anna retreated to the kitchen.

Katie knew she should do something, but she wasn't quite sure what. Levi Bender was still standing, and Melody and her mother were staring at each other warily, almost like dogs on the street . . . sizing each other up.

While Katie struggled to think of something to say, anything appropriate, her mother broke the silence. "So, Melody, I have to admit that I didn't expect to receive two guests today."

The lines around her lips tightened. "You didn't?"

"No. Are you here by chance? Are . . . you lost, miss?"

"Not at all."

The girl answered politely, but there seemed to be much that she wasn't saying. Katie didn't appreciate that. Though they hosted many guests at their bed-and-breakfast, the inn was also her home. She didn't appreciate housing someone who was in the habit of lying. "I have to tell you, we don't have a record of your reservation. Your appearance is something of a shock." As was her condition. And her fainting.

She blinked. "That is surprising. I'm sure I made a reservation."

Katie now knew she was lying. "When did you call?"

"Last week sometime? I spoke with a . . . man."

That was yet another signal that the girl was telling stories. Rarely did her father or Henry answer the phone.

"Did you, now?" Katie asked sarcastically as irritation filled her. This girl had a lot of nerve, to appear in their yard on the twentieth of December, lying through her teeth! "Do you, by any chance, happen to remember this man's name?"

"No . . ."

"Are you sure?"

"Katie, go into the pantry and bring out some peanut butter cookies," her mother said sharply.

Katie immediately complied. But as she left the room, avoiding the constant glare of Mr. Bender, Katie heard her mother's gasp. "Oh, my. You're going to have a baby!"

As the girl murmured something in return, Katie stumbled. Why in the world would a girl be coming to the inn by herself at Christmas?

And where was Melody's family? Her husband?

And why was she traveling, anyway? When she'd been that far along with Eli, the midwife had cautioned Katie from doing anything too strenuous at all. And Jonathan had been beside himself with worry, coming home each day from the lumber mill at noon just to check on her.

So how come Melody's man had let her go? And if he had . . . of all the places in the world . . . why had she settled upon their inn?

Just five days before Christmas Day?

Chapter 3

December 20, 4:30 P.M.

The feeling that had been boiling inside of Levi from the moment he'd seen the three women walking in the snow increased tenfold. Now, instead of just being empty and listless, emotions he'd carefully tamped down months ago surged forward with a vengeance.

Anger. Despair. Worry. Shame. Guilt. It was all coming back.

Coming here had been a mistake.

Already the Brenneman Bed and Breakfast felt too confining. Too warm. Too homey. Too close. He ached for anonymity the way most others yearned for acceptance. He most certainly did not want to be sitting in the family's private parlor drinking coffee and eating cookies.

He'd resisted, of course. When the pretty blonde brought

in a tray of refreshments, Levi attempted to escape. But Mrs. Brenneman would not take no for an answer. Before he knew it, he was seated across from her, holding a thick mug of piping hot coffee.

At least, he mused, they weren't paying too much attention to him. No, all their focus was pinned firmly on the petite girl with auburn hair who looked no older than twenty years of age.

But it wasn't her age that frightened him. It was the fact that she was heavy with child.

As he continued to sip his coffee, the other women fussed and asked questions. As she haltingly murmured that she'd come all the way from Kentucky, and that her baby was due in three weeks' time, Levi felt his skin flush with embarrassment.

The women acted like this was a usual thing, to discuss pregnancies with complete strangers. Worse, the proprietor, Mrs. Brenneman, acted like they were all about to become fast friends.

He would not.

Fact was, he had not come to the inn in order to make new friends. He had come to wait out the holiday as best he could. He did not want to get to know the Brennemans, and he most certainly didn't want to get to know Melody. Even just looking at a woman heavy with child brought back too many painful memories.

Regret for his decision to escape to the Brennemans' filled him. For some reason, he'd imagined that the inn would be filled to the seams with guests, not filled to the seams with family.

The Lord had surely wasted no time in proving to him that it wasn't possible to avoid feelings and responsibilities and hurts. They always came back.

Like His presence, they were always there. Lurking among the depths. Waiting to be acknowledged.

He wished he had a way to leave. For the first time in a long while he wished for a driver's license. For a car of his own. Then he'd be able to escape. Never had he imagined that he'd be surrounded by so many women.

"Is your coffee all right?" the blond woman asked, disrupting his thoughts.

"It's fine." When she looked pleased and stood up, he stared at the heavy ceramic mug in front of him curiously. The liquid inside was rich-looking and dark. Now that he noticed, the aroma of a superior blend wafted toward him, teasing his senses. Had he taken a sip yet? He didn't remember.

Though he hoped the woman would take a hint by his brusque manner and leave him in peace, she soon appeared again. In her hands was a blue stoneware plate filled with soft peanut butter cookies and generous slices of iced cranberry bread.

With a bit of a flourish, she presented it with a smile. "Please have some bread, if you'd care to. I made it fresh this morning."

He took a piece because he didn't have a choice. It was still warm. The faint scent of tangy cranberries, walnuts, and sugar drifted toward him—reminding him of just how long it had been since he'd had anything fresh from the oven.

Not since Rosanna. As expected, the realization made his stomach knot. There was no way he'd ever be able to eat a bite; yet somewhere in the depths of his psyche, good manners reared up.

It would be rude not to eat even a little of the food. But perhaps he could take it to his room and find a way to dispose of it later? "I'm ready to see to my room. Is it ready?"

"It is, but please don't hurry on our account." Not looking perturbed in the slightest by his awkward manner, she smiled serenely. "Please, just relax and enjoy your snack. That's why you're here, right? To relax?"

He was there to forget. To hide.

When he looked at her, confused, she flushed prettily. "I'm sorry if we seem out of sorts. But it can't be helped, actually. We only received your reservation today!"

"Today?"

"Yes. There was a problem with the delivery, I guess. Anyway, I know things are a little chaotic now, but we'll get it all settled soon enough."

Levi figured that by "a little chaotic," she was referring to the pregnant girl who'd fainted.

"Now, where are you from?"

"Berlin."

"My. That's quite a ways."

"Long enough."

"Was your trip all right?"

"There were no problems."

"Do you have family there?"

"Some."

"But no wife?"

Her voice was melodic. Her tone hopeful. He felt like she was beating him with a stick, though. Each intrusive comment made him shudder. "I have no wife," he finally said.

She grinned. "I didn't imagine so." At his look of shock, she chuckled. "I'm sorry. I mean, no wife I know of would let you leave at Christmas!"

The proper thing to do would be to at least smile at her horrible attempt at a joke. The polite thing to do would be to try harder to make senseless small talk.

But as her voice rang in his head—as her words reverberated, reminding him again that his Rosanna had died at Christmas—Levi felt ill.

The table shook in his haste to stand up. "Excuse me," he murmured, then trotted out to the front porch. To the cold, cold air.

At least there he could concentrate on the wind and snow to chill his features. To calm his reserve.

To let him try to figure out what in the world he'd been thinking . . . when he'd decided to escape his life for Christmas.

Obviously, no matter where he went and no matter how hard he tried, there would be no escape from his guilt.

Ever.

Chapter 4

December 20, 5:00 P.M.

The movements in her belly were called Braxton Hicks contractions. That's all they are, Melody told herself as she lay on her side in the middle of the queen-sized bed in her room. But as the muscles in her stomach squeezed again, and she shifted uncomfortably, Melody wondered how much different *real* contractions felt.

Because these, she decided, felt terribly real to her.

Breathe, she told herself. Breathe deep. That was the mantra she had repeated to herself for the last nine months. Ever since "it" had happened. Ever since she'd been attacked and violated by the side of the road on her way home from work.

As Melody slowly inhaled, counted one Mississippi, two

Mississippi, and then exhaled, her body seemed to relax slightly. And the burdensome stress that had become her constant companion eased. Little by little, she felt her shoulders loosen, then the muscles in her back and hips stretch and give way. Finally the cramping lessened and the baby seemed to settle inside her again.

She was not going to have a baby today. Closing her eyes, Melody said a prayer of thanks.

Thanks for her body's newfound patience, and for all her blessings. Yes, that was what she needed to do. She needed to get her bearings and feel good about herself again. She needed this little vacation, this time of rest, more than she'd ever needed anything in her life. Shifting, she moved to her other side and pulled one of the fluffy down pillows closer to her chest. The scent of starch and detergent drifted forth, smelling fresh and clean.

Reminding Melody of how wonderful-*gut* it was to be in such lovely surroundings.

Soon after she'd gotten her bearings, Mrs. Brenneman had walked her to her guest room . . . a beautiful room decorated in blues and whites on the first floor, right behind the main sitting area. Because getting off her feet had sounded so wonderful, she ignored her feelings of unease as Mrs. Brenneman wished her a good rest, paused to look at her in concern again, and then quietly shut the door behind her.

And she had a lot to be uneasy about. So far, everything about the inn had been different than what she'd imagined. The family living in and managing the inn were far more nosy than she'd anticipated. It was also extremely obvious they weren't all that excited to have her stay with them. If Katie had been able to send their uninvited guest on her way, she surely would have. During every encounter, Katie had been especially scornful. It felt as if there was nothing Melody could do about that attitude, either.

Except to leave.

And then there was the other guest. Levi Bender. A lone man who obviously was harboring some secrets of his own. Plus, he was so sullen, it looked as if the very act of smiling would cause him pain. What could have happened to him? Melody wondered. He'd actually paled when he saw she was pregnant.

The right thing to do might have been to go back home, but of course she couldn't do that. Her parents and May, her sister, had argued so much about her leaving that they would no doubt do their best to remind her of their wisdom time and again. Their attitudes would surely make a difficult holiday even worse.

And they wouldn't let her just sit in her room alone, either. No, they'd expect her to help prepare supper and wash dishes, just like any good daughter. Complaints about being tired would be ignored. Worries verbalized about her future would be met with silence.

The only option was to pretend that everything was just fine while she was here. That she didn't notice that she wasn't wanted at the inn.

Because at least here, she would be safe. The man who had attacked her was far away. Maybe she'd get a welcome break from the nightmares that plagued her. From the memories that crushed her heart and wouldn't allow her to forget for even the smallest second what it had felt like to be assaulted by the stranger.

Of how his rough fingers had scraped her skin. Of how the hospital's strong antiseptic scent had burned her nose. How the nurses' voices had been strained and hushed when they spoke to the doctors. Of how the English doctors had talked about so much that she didn't understand.

A tear escaped as she closed her eyes. Breathing deep, she caught the scent of freshly made gingerbread and held it close. It smelled heavenly and warm. Like a childhood memory that existed only in her dreams.

Breathe in. Breathe out. Think of better days. Of other times.

Think only of what a perfect holiday should smell like. Think of cinnamon and molasses. Of fresh snow. Of what she used to feel like. Before.

Little by little, she felt her body relax once again. Maybe this time she'd be able to take a nap.

"I still don't see why we are obligated to let them both stay here," Katie whispered as she rushed to help her mother pull out a handful of vegetables for soup. "The girl doesn't have a reservation. She even admitted to not even trying to make one. And there's something peculiar about her. Actually, there's something strange about that man, too. He had less conversation inside him than this chair right here."

"He is quiet," her mother agreed, "but we've had other guests who were quiet, too. There's nothing wrong with that."

"I suppose. Well, if he only wants to be left alone, that won't be difficult. But that girl is another story. She definitely should not have shown up like she did. Without a reservation. We could point that out to her."

While her mother only turned on the sink and began scrubbing carrots, it was her brother Henry who chided her. "She's with child. If she's here alone, it's obvious she has nowhere else to go. You can't *not* allow her to stay."

Put that way, Katie felt ashamed. But not enough to give up her fight for the perfect holiday. Unbidden, tears sparked her eyes, which was a terribly curious thing.

Obviously, her emotions were running high. Too high to be reasonable.

But before her brain could caution her tongue, she started talking again. "But why do you think she's here? She's awfully big. Close to her time, don't you think? Too close to travel."

"Neither you nor I is her doctor. It doesn't matter what we think."

"It does. What if something goes wrong?" Alarm coursed through her as Katie started to imagine all sorts of worst-case scenarios. "What if she needs a physician on Christmas Eve? What would we do then?"

"Then we'll find a doctor. Accidents happen all the time, but God always provides," Henry said reasonably.

But Katie didn't want to be reasonable. She wanted to be surrounded just by her family and friends this holiday. She was tired and Eli had been challenging. All that had gotten her through the last couple of weeks was looking forward to spending the holiday together.

But now her dreams were disappearing. "What if she's on the run from her husband? She could bring danger here."

As a shadow filled Henry's eyes, Katie felt her cheeks flush. But still, her mouth kept running on. "I'm sorry. I know you're thinking of when Anna hid here, but this is different."

"Perhaps. Or perhaps not . . ."

"If she is in trouble, then she's brought it our way. And I, for one, don't think that's right. I have Eli."

As her last plaintive objection filled the air, her mother whirled around and glared. "Enough, Katie. Your talk is shameful. I don't want to hear another word against our guests again."

"Yes, Mamm."

"It's time you looked beyond yourself, Katie, and think about other people's needs instead of your own. You should consider the Lord's wishes, too."

"But—"

"You might not have heard, but there was another woman, years ago, who asked for a room in an inn near December twenty-fifth. Imagine how much nicer it would have been for her if she'd been given shelter."

"Mother, I see the similarities, but no matter what you say, I'll not be persuaded that Melody Gingerich is just like Mary."

"Then you listen to this, daughter. You've been so short-tempered, I'm half tempted to send you back to your home. You ought to think about why the Lord has brought these two people to us. Obviously, He intended for them to be here. It's too coincidental otherwise. The roads are snowy and most folks are canceling their travel plans."

Her mother's words stilled all further complaints. She did have a point. Perhaps there was a reason for them to have visitors. Perhaps these two guests really did have a greater need to be with their family than the rest of them did to be alone. "I'm sorry. I'll try to be better."

Her mother arched a brow. "Try?"

"I will be better. I promise."

Now that she'd been obeyed, her tone gentled. "That Melody needs a friend, Katie. I imagine she's worried about the baby and being a mother. You just had Eli a few months ago. You should reach out to her and offer her your friendship. Perhaps she doesn't have much of a family. Perhaps she has no one. Katie, what would your life be like if you didn't have any of us?"

Her mother's question caused a rush of fear. She loved her family dearly. And Jonathan? Well, Jonathan was the best husband for her, even discounting the fact she'd loved him from afar for years before he'd ever turned her way. He was patient with her, and offered a lot of support when she was worried. And his girls had given her so much, too.

Life without them would be a dark thing, indeed.

"You won't hear me complain or whine again, Mamm."

But instead of looking pleased, her mother and brother chuckled.

"To hear you not whine would be the greatest Christmas gift of all," Henry quipped.

Instead of snipping at him right back, Katie smiled

sweetly. "Please hand me the sack of potatoes, brother. I'll do my best not to grumble about your unusually large appetite."

December 21, 7:00 A.M.

Leah Dillon wasn't quite sure why she felt so strongly about following her friend Melody to the bed-and-breakfast, but she did. Actually, she knew she wasn't going to be able to think about anything other than her friend's health and well-being if she didn't go see Melody herself.

Looking around her room, decorated like she was perpetually sixteen in shades of violet and cream, she checked again to see if she'd forgotten anything.

Not that it mattered. With luck, she'd be home again by Christmas. Hefting her backpack on her right shoulder, she turned off her light and headed into the kitchen where her mother was waiting, the twinkling white lights of their Christmas tree casting a pretty glow around her. "I think that's everything. I guess I'm ready, Mom."

"I guess you are." She handed her three twenty-dollar bills. "Take this, okay?"

Leah kept her hand securely in her pocket. "I won't need that, Mom. I cashed my last paycheck."

"Go ahead and take it. You never know what could happen."

But Leah knew they didn't have a lot of extra cash. Not for extras, or for spur-of-the-moment trips like the one she was about to take. Leah was pretty sure if she took the cash, her mother would be eating peanut butter and jelly sandwiches for the next four days. "Really, Mom. I'll be fine."

"If you don't use it, bring it back." She looked her over once again. "Do you have enough warm clothes?"

"I've got boots, turtlenecks, jeans, and socks. Even fresh underwear," Leah added, just to make her mom smile. "Trust me, I'll be warm enough."

"And you have your cell phone?"

"I do. And the charger, too." She smiled. "Have I told you thanks for not giving me too much grief for doing this?"

"You're twenty-one, Leah. It's not like I could stop you."

While their relationship was far more like that of roommates than mother and child, Leah felt her mom still deserved every courtesy. Especially since she'd been so good about letting Leah remain at home while she finished up her degree and worked at Great Grinds. "Well, still. Thanks. You're the best."

"You're welcome." A weary smile brightened up her mother's pale cheeks. "Besides, there's no need to thank me." Her mom chuckled as she reached out and hugged Leah tightly, enfolding her in an embrace as familiar as the scent of Ivory soap that always clung to her. "I don't know if I'm the best, but I do understand why you need to go. Melody shouldn't be all alone right now."

"She left yesterday morning without a word to anyone," Leah said as she pulled away. "When Mrs. Sheridan told me Melody was going to Ohio all by herself, I couldn't believe it."

"I know you were surprised," her mother replied in her typical understated way. "Don't forget that this was Melody's decision, though. You need to respect that."

"I do. But I don't know if she's made an informed decision."

"Informed?" Grinning, she tilted her head to one side. "Leah, are you throwing that phrase out at me for any special reason?"

"Only because it was your favorite phrase when I was fifteen."

As she always did whenever they mentioned that very difficult year, her mom winced dramatically. "I only said 'informed' all the time because you never seemed to want to think about consequences. Ever."

"I do now." Reaching out, she clasped her mother's hand. "I just don't want Melody to be alone, you know? She's had such a tough time."

"No one has ever denied that. But, remember what we talked about? I know you're studying to be a guidance counselor, but you can't live someone else's life, Leah. Melody is Amish, not like us. And her parents love her and want the best for her . . . even if they've behaved in ways that you don't agree with."

Thinking of how Melody had practically lived in shame for the last nine months made Leah cringe. "They've been awful."

"Maybe so, but it's not for us to interfere."

"I can't just stay here." As she looked at her mom, with her straight brown hair and brown eyes, with her delicate jaw and skin that never wanted to tan—all features that she'd inherited—Leah struggled to put all her thoughts into words. "You're my best friend. You've always had my back. I don't think Melody's ever had that."

"So you need to be there for her."

"Yes. I know she's hurting." As every worst-case scenario filtered through her mind, Leah steadied her resolve. "And I know when someone's hurting they don't always make the best choices."

"They also don't have the best responses when someone tries to do something nice for them. Don't be surprised if she's not thrilled to see you," she added as they walked into the small living room.

In addition to the sparkling tree, two stockings hung from the mantel and a whole assortment of snow globes and music boxes filled every available space.

"I won't be." However, inside, Leah was sure her mom was wrong about Melody. No matter what, she knew her friend was going to be thrilled to see her. "It's going to be fine. If she wants to stay, I'll stay there with her. And, if she's regretting her decision to go to the middle of no-where for Christmas, well, I'll just take her home."

"I hope it will be that easy."

"It will be. She needs a friend," Leah added, knowing she spoke the truth. "Melody needs me. And she needs to continue to talk. She's kept so much inside—sometimes I worry. No matter how many times I've asked her what she's thinking, she never will say anything but that she's fine."

"Leah—Oh, never mind." Her mother's voice broke off as she again enfolded her daughter in her arms. Tenderly, she kissed her head. "You're a good person."

Leah fiercely hugged her mother back. "I wish her mom was more like you. I wish her mom would have reached out to her more."

"I know." She shook her head sadly. "Sometimes I just don't understand people. Never would I have imagined that a parent could be so uncaring. It certainly wasn't Melody's fault she was attacked."

"If you acted that way to me, why, I just don't know what I'd do. Probably go off the deep end." As she visualized how empty her life would be, without her mother's love and support, Leah reached out her hand. "Mom, I hope that's not what's been happening to Melody."

As her mother clasped her hand, she shook her head. "Nope. I'm not going to let you go there. Let's think positively. You're going to get to the inn tonight. You're going to visit with her, and spend the night there."

"And stay another day or two."

"And then you're going to come right back, with plenty of time to celebrate Christmas Day."

"Yep. And if Melody wants to stay with us, she's more than welcome."

"Of course. Well, is your car full of gas?"

"Yes." She stepped closer to the door—anxious to leave, but not. This trip was a big deal for her. Never had she driven so far by herself. Never had she taken a chance like the one she was taking now.

"Then, I guess you better go. The sooner you leave, the sooner you'll come home."

Leah grabbed the door's handle but didn't turn it. "I'll call you tonight."

"You better. Good-bye, dear. Have a good trip, and be careful."

"I will. And Mom . . . I hope you won't be too lonely."

"I have my books and the dogs. That's enough for me. Now, it's time, Leah."

Leah hugged her mom again and hustled to her sedan. She tossed her pack in the backseat and started the car.

She was going on an adventure. And though it really wasn't much of one . . . after all, all she was doing was checking up on Melody and then coming back . . . Leah couldn't wait.

Things in her life had been pretty boring lately. All she'd been doing was working at Great Grinds and taking classes in counseling at the community college. It was time for excitement.

But as she drove down her street, and her house and her mom's silhouette faded into the background, Leah wondered if she was about to get more than she bargained for.

As the doubts settled in again, she turned up the radio. It did as she hoped—blocked everything in the world out.

For better or worse, she was on her way.

Chapter 5

December 21, 10:00 A.M.

"I hope I didn't disturb you."

Melody looked up at the man who stood at the doorway of the parlor. Levi Bender. Her eyes flew to his hand, which was gripping the oak doorframe like he was in danger of falling.

Of course, it was so obvious that his balance wasn't in question, it was his comfort level. Though whether he was worried more about hers or his, she didn't know. "You didn't disturb me. I was simply enjoying the fire."

"Oh."

His reticence was almost laughable. He seemed as awkward around her as she usually felt around most strangers. Most of the time, men who were muscular reminded her too much of the man who had attacked her. Who raped her.

But Levi felt different. As he hovered nearby, an unusual kind of awareness pulsed through her. He was a handsome man. His dark hair and eyes tempted her to look at him a little too long. A little too closely.

Not to look away. How could that be?

When he continued to pause at the door, obviously debating whether to join her or not, she sighed. "Please join me, if you'd like. The fire feels *gut*, and there's a carafe of coffee on the back table."

A spark of interest flashed in his eyes. *"Kaffi?"*

"It's fresh. You might as well come on in and enjoy yourself. Don't let me deter you. It's not like this is my place. After all, we are both guests here, *jah*?"

After another moment's hesitation, he stepped inside. As she half expected, he walked right over and poured a mug of hot coffee. What she didn't expect was to see him liberally add sugar and cream to it. What had necessitated that? she wondered. To her surprise, she fought off a smile when he sipped, then added still more cream to it. He was obviously a man who liked his sweets. Then she wondered why she even cared.

Once his coffee was mixed, Levi stood awkwardly once again. Looking terribly ill at ease.

Because he still stayed silent—and because the continued strain was starting to get on her nerves—she raised her hands to the fire. "The fireplace really does feel comforting."

He raised a brow at the word.

"I mean, the house is warm, but it still contains drafts. I was thankful for the featherbed last night." She didn't even bother to say it helped her sleep, because it hadn't.

Nothing really helped that.

"Mr. Brenneman said their home has been in their family for a few generations."

Though his statement was spoken awkwardly, she grabbed on to his words like a lifeline. "That's nice, huh?" When his expression stayed blank, she hastened to explain. "I mean, my parents moved to their house soon after I was born. I imagine it would be nice to live somewhere where there are memories of grandparents in every corner."

"I don't know about that." He swallowed. "Some memories are too hard to think about."

"Yes. You're right." There was no way she was going to dispute that statement. Some memories were far too painful to free from the locked box of her mind. If she had her way, she'd wish to never recall some things ever again.

He held his hands up. "The fire does feel good. I could have used a warm spot like this yesterday. It was a cold day to travel."

"Did you come from very far?"

"A fair amount. Took me most of the day," he added.

"It took me most of the day as well."

"You traveled some distance, too?"

Melody didn't fail to notice that his question was asked grudgingly, like only good manners necessitated that he inquire. He'd also given her a question that could be neatly sidestepped as well.

All she'd have to do is give him a one-word answer and they could consider the conversation over.

But for all of his gruffness, she felt safer with him than she had with any man in months. Feeling brave and almost chatty, she said, "I came all the way from Kentucky. From Sonora, which is south of Louisville. Do you know it?"

"*Nee.*"

"Well, it's a ways away, especially in this weather." She shivered dramatically. "It was a long journey."

"Perhaps it was too long. After all, you collapsed when you arrived."

She couldn't escape his disapproval. She also couldn't escape what had happened. "I feel better now."

But instead of commenting on her health, he stepped closer. "Why, exactly, are you here?"

"Pardon me?" A tremor flitted inside her. Perhaps this man wasn't so harmless after all.

Those dark eyes of his seemed to miss nothing as he stared. Immediately, she noticed the stain on her gray dress. The cracked skin on her finger from the cold. With a sinking sensation, she imagined that he was examining the dark circles under her eyes that seemed to never go away.

And, of course, her protruding stomach.

"You look like you could give birth at any moment. Surely this trip you've taken was foolhardy. Most likely, it wasn't safe for the babe. But still you went."

She wrapped her arms around herself. "The baby is fine."

"As far as you know . . ." Something dark entered his eyes. "Whyever would you decide to take such a risk with your baby's health? And why in the world are you alone?"

Melody realized then that she'd been hopelessly naive. Of course men had more ways to hurt than with their hands! The lashing of questions felt as wounding as any hard-ironed grip.

In a panic, she was tempted to make up lies. To say something about her husband dying. Or that he was with an ailing parent and so had encouraged her to go to the inn.

Anything that would be socially acceptable, even if thought to be strange. But she'd been caught in lies so often lately, she didn't dare.

Lies meant that you had to remember things. And she had no willpower for that at the moment. In fact, she was fairly sure she would completely forget just about everything the moment she'd said a word. That was how it had been going lately, anyway.

So she evaded. Again. "I don't believe the reason I'm here is anyone's business."

"I think otherwise." His voice was harsh, and the look he gave her made her shudder. "You have put everyone here in a state of worry."

"I certainly have not. Who said such a thing?"

He paused. "What if you need medical assistance?"

Ah, it looked like she wasn't the only one who could dodge questions. "If I did, I don't see how that would be your concern."

"I'd never be able to stand by while a woman needed help."

She wondered why he was even thinking about such things.

"We are strangers. I promise you, if I need help, I certainly won't be calling for you."

Irritation emanated from him.

Which pricked her temper even further. With effort, she fought to keep her voice low and even. She didn't want to risk showing too much of her emotions to this man. No doubt, he would use her weaknesses as fodder for another barb later. "Well, I'm not quite sure why the Lord brought us here together. Perhaps it was simply chance."

"Our Lord makes no accidents."

Melody imagined he was right. But there was something about his sanctimonious tone that riled her up in a way only the prim ladies who said they were friends with her mother could.

Those ladies had done everything they could to make sure she knew she wasn't worthy enough to cross their paths.

And this man . . . this dark-haired, dark-eyed, angry man—why, he acted like he was just as dismayed.

She cleared her throat. "Mr. Bender. We only happen to be here for a short while. I suggest we try our best to be civil to each other. After all, by the time the new year comes, we both will be gone. And after that, why, I'm sure our paths will likely never cross again."

"I sincerely hope they do not."

The tension between them increased. Melody considered leaving the room in a huff. She was mad enough and certainly had no desire to see him. But there was nowhere to go, save her room. And though the featherbed and comforters would keep her snug during the night, it was a far sight chillier in her room than where she was sitting.

Almost as chilly as the glare he was sending her way. And that, of course, made her completely confused. He seemed like the type of man who did his best to stay away from people who he didn't like. To stay away from opinions he didn't share.

Inside her, emotions clashed and battled with each other. Part of her wanted nothing better than to move away from Levi and sit by herself. But a whole different side yearned for the thrill she got from conversing with him. He challenged her in a way that wasn't hard-hearted or scary. Instead, he seemed to treat her as an equal. Not someone damaged by life.

No one else had treated her in such a way. As the battle of wills played out, she wondered who would be the victor. She'd already sat by herself for hours. She knew what that felt like.

And, just as she knew that she didn't care for spinach . . . or that nothing could make her smile like a daffodil in springtime . . . she knew this time with Levi would end eventually.

And with it, her only chance to converse like someone who was strong. Not afraid of life.

"Why did you come to a bed-and-breakfast for Christmas, anyway? It seems to me a man such as yourself would have a lot of family around."

"A man such as myself?"

"You know. So pleasant. So gregarious." She felt the bite of satisfaction when he visibly winced. "I'm sure all your relatives tried hard to convince you to stay."

"They did. I was eager to be alone, though."

Obviously, he, too, had his own reasons for wanting to be at the inn. She felt ashamed. She shouldn't have goaded him like that. There was no reason for her to have egged him on so. He owed her nothing. And surely, her behavior wasn't Christian.

Her palms started to sweat. She, more than anyone, knew all about wishing to just get along. To simply have a conversation with another person without feeling judged. Or without feeling like she needed to explain herself. "I'm sorry," she began. "I shouldn't have—"

"Here you both are," Mrs. Brenneman exclaimed as she bustled inside. "How are you two doing? Did you have a good night's sleep? Have you settled in?"

"I slept well." After a long moment, Levi turned from Melody and smiled at their host. "My room is comfortable."

"Mine is as well," Melody mumbled. "The quilts adorning the walls and covering the beds are lovely."

"Let's just hope they keep you warm, *jah*? It's terribly cold outside."

"I'm sure they will."

Mrs. Brenneman's smile broadened. "Well, don't mind me. I only came in here to check on the two of you. My Anna told me she fixed you breakfast, and I see you've found coffee as well."

"It has all been *wunderbaar*."

"I'm delighted to hear that. And, I see that you both are getting to know each other, too! How nice."

Melody couldn't think of a thing to say to that.

Oblivious to their discomfort, Mrs. Brenneman clasped her hands together in front of her. "If you two don't mind, I thought I'd warn you about all of our goings-on this week."

"What do you mean?"

"As it so happens, my whole family will be arriving to stay over the next two days. We'll be baking cookies and chopping wood and working on a puzzle. It should be great fun." Each word was punctuated with joy and happiness . . . and an iron will.

Melody was beginning to realize that Mrs. Brenneman was not a lady used to having her wishes ignored.

But why was the innkeeper telling her such things, anyway? The activities were most definitely geared toward her family, not guests.

Levi's shoulders sagged. "I'll do my best to stay out of your way."

"No! No, that's not why I am telling you! We want you to join in!" She looked at them both. "Idle hands make fretful minds, I think. And I also think you'll enjoy things if you just jump in with both feet. You do know how to chop wood, don't you, Levi?"

"Of course."

"And Melody, I trust you've made a fair share of Christmas cookies before?"

"Yes."

"Then it's settled. I want you two to become part of our family while you're here."

"But I'm sure I don't want to be any trouble," Levi said.

"You won't be, if you participate. It's folks who are determined to be alone and standoffish that are hard for us. Then we have to constantly be wondering what they need."

She patted Levi on the arm. "So please meet my son Henry outside in fifteen minutes. He and my husband and whoever else shows up are going for a hike. I fully expect you men to either come back with wood or a turkey."

"I'll be there."

"And me, Mrs. Brenneman?"

"Melody, we want you to help hold Eli while we bake."

"Katie's baby?"

"Yes, of course. You'll want the practice with the baby, yes?"

There seemed to be no other answer but one of agreement. She nodded.

"I'm glad that's all settled," Mrs. Brenneman said before leaving.

"I'm not sure what just happened, but I think we've been put to work." Melody looked Levi's way again, wondering if he was ever going to show some kind of reaction.

But still, his face remained impassive. "Yes."

The silence between them stretched, growing even more uncomfortable. With effort, she lumbered to her feet. "I'll just go to the kitchen now," Melody murmured, not really knowing why she even said that much. After all, he certainly didn't look like he cared one way or another.

So she left—making sure that she didn't even think about turning around to see his reaction.

Though, knowing him, he probably hadn't even noticed she was gone.

* * *

December 21, 10:15 A.M.

After what had felt like an eternity, she left. When he no longer could hear her footsteps on the thick wooden planks, Levi exhaled. Finally, it felt like he could breathe again.

As the flames jumped and popped in the fire, Levi took the time to wonder why such a girl affected him so. It certainly wasn't her beauty. She was full with child—another man's child. And she was young, too. Too young for marriage, in his estimation.

She was too forward by half as well. Levi had always enjoyed quiet women. A woman who didn't mind the silence. She acted like silence was simply an opportunity to fill the air with chatter.

So what was it that kept him thinking about her again and again? Even now, when he truly ached for her to leave him?

It had to be her eyes. They were sad. So sad and full of grief that their expression took his breath away.

Probably because he knew such desolation.

Henry poked his head into the room. "Levi, my *mamm* says you'd like to come with us. Is that the case?"

He scrambled to his feet. "Did you think it wasn't?"

"She's been known to push her ways on us a time or two. We would be happy to have you join us, though, if you want."

"I want to," he replied, suddenly realizing that he did

not want to be outside in the company of men. "I'll be right there."

"Good. We'll meet in the barn."

As Levi climbed the flights of stairs to his room, for a moment he was sure he heard the women's voices raised in laughter. In spite of himself, he found himself straining to hear their words. Women were so different than men. They talked of things he never noticed, discussed ideas he never thought about.

Funny how all of a sudden he missed that. He missed being around laughter and the easy chatter of women.

And as he met Henry, his father John, Jonathan Lundy, and another man, Samuel, and they all tromped off toward the east, two carrying rifles, Levi found his shoulders relaxing.

How long had it been since no one had asked how he was feeling? How long had it been since no one had walked on eggshells around him?

Since no one cared about his past?

Chapter 6

December 21, 12:00 P.M.

"Anna, here," Katie said to Melody, "was once English. She's far more worldly than the rest of us." Katie's eyebrows rose in amusement.

To her left, Anna shook her head in dismay. "I don't know why you always feel the need to speak of my past, Katie. That's ancient history."

Across the room, another girl, Winnie, chuckled. "So ancient, it happened two years ago."

Anna lifted her chin. "Well, it feels ancient."

Melody watched the interaction among the three women with a great deal of envy. They had a bond she'd only dreamed of having with other women. A bond she'd never come close to experiencing with her own sister. In fact, the only person she felt she could even feel such a connection with was Leah.

But even that relationship had begun to change, though it was through no fault of Leah's. No, it had been her doing. Little by little, she'd been pulling away from her co-worker. Leah was pretty, with a vibrant personality and a bright future.

Melody had none of that. Soon, their lives would be even more dissimilar. She would have a baby and be struggling to make ends meet. Leah, on the other hand, would be leaving their small Kentucky town for good as soon as she received her college degree.

She would start a career and become friends with other English girls doing the same thing. There would be no cause for her to keep in touch with someone so different.

But at the moment, as she longingly watched the exchanges between the ladies in the Brennemans' kitchen, Melody started to reevaluate her feelings. Perhaps she'd shied away from Leah too quickly. Perhaps the right thing to do would have been to let Leah decide whether or not to continue to be her friend? After all, the trio of girls in front of her didn't seem too much alike.

And yet these women weren't sisters at all. Only sisters of their hearts. Daring to enter the conversation, she said, "Tell me how you came to be Amish, then, Anna. That is, if you don't mind."

"It's a long story," Anna said as she scooped up a handful of flour and spread it around the wooden butcher block table. Melody knew Anna was making pretzels.

"I don't mind a long story, that is, if you want to tell it."

"Well, it all started when I was little. My mom took me here for a weekend to learn to quilt and Katie and I hit it off."

"We became pen pals," Katie added.

Melody tried to imagine the chain of events. "You became such good friends that you decided to become Amish?"

Anna laughed. "No. I never planned to ever be Amish." A shadow entered her eyes. "Actually, I planned to marry well and be a housewife. But the man I was dating turned out to be a pretty bad guy."

Winnie, who was frying hamburger for a casserole, widened her eyes. "He was a *verra* bad man, Anna. He beat you."

Little Eli frowned as Melody gripped him too hard. "Sorry," she murmured, cuddling him closer. Once the baby was sleeping contentedly again, she glanced Anna's way. "You were beaten?"

A shadow filled Anna's beautiful green eyes. "I . . . was. Not all the time, and not at first . . . but it slowly was getting worse. I was scared."

Remembering how it had felt to be helpless, Melody shivered. "I imagine you were."

Anna was rolling the dough into long strips with her palms. Quickly, she lifted her head and looked Melody's way. When their eyes met, Melody felt a new awareness pass between them. They both knew what it felt like to be a victim.

Then Anna cleared her throat. "Anyway, he was an important guy and I didn't think anyone would help me. So I came here for help."

"She hid here," Katie said. "She wore my clothes and

pretended to be Amish. We practically lived on pins and needles, worried she would be found."

"But along the way, Anna fell in love with my Henry," Mrs. Brenneman said, bustling in the room with a smile. "And then it was just a matter of time before everything worked out."

Never had Melody heard such a story. "I have an English friend, but I can't imagine her ever wanting to become Amish."

"I would have loved Anna even if she had stayed in the outside world. But now she's married to my brother and we are truly sisters, and I'm terribly grateful."

Anna looked at Katie fondly. "I feel the same way. I grew up as an only child, so now having Katie and Winnie, it's a wonderful thing."

Winnie looked at Melody and grinned. "I am Jonathan's sister. Jonathan Lundy is Katie's husband."

"And you are married, too?"

"I am. I married Samuel Miller. He grew up with us."

"Ah, so you've known him for some time," Melody said, enjoying all the other girls' romances.

A spark entered Winnie's gray eyes. "That is mostly true. But Sam was an *Englischer* for a time—a professor at a college. We only got reacquainted when I was in the hospital."

Anna smiled at Winnie fondly. "Winnie was injured when Jonathan and Katie's barn burned down."

"My word!"

"Oh, I ended up all right," Winnie reassured her as she held up her arm. Melody noticed a faint discoloration marking her forearm. "Now all I have is a few reminders of that event."

"And Samuel," Katie said. "We can't forget him!"

Mrs. Brenneman laughed with the girls. Melody couldn't help but smile as well.

She was charmed by the other girls, and pleased that they shared so much with her. In Melody's experience, people didn't accept newcomers. And people really didn't accept bad things that came. For most, it was far better to pretend those things didn't exist. To push them out of their lives, so they didn't have to see them.

Didn't have to deal with them.

Anna chuckled. "I'm sorry. Did I shock you?"

"Nee." Melody struggled to put into words everything she was thinking. "I just never imagined someone could make a change like that."

"It wasn't easy, but I had a lot of help."

It took everything she had to keep her voice even and calm. To act like she was merely curious about Anna's past, not trying to learn from it. "What happened to the man?"

"The man who beat me?" she asked slowly.

Melody nodded, afraid to speak.

"Actually, he kept looking for me. For weeks. And then, when he discovered where I was, he came after me."

"He came here. To our house," Katie supplied. Melody watched her hands grip her rolling pin, the only indication of how scary that visit must have been.

Anna nodded, all traces of humor gone from her face. "It was really scary. The whole time I was petrified. I didn't want to get hurt, but most of all, I didn't want any of the Brennemans to get hurt."

Katie folded her arms over her chest. "We weren't helpless. We were ready to defend her."

"I don't know," Anna allowed. "It was a difficult time. I was hiding out here, pretending to be something I wasn't; falling in love with Henry, yet always worried that Rob was going to appear at the door at any minute."

"But your parents?"

"I'm sorry to say I didn't trust them enough to tell them where I was." Her voice drifted off for a moment. Then Anna shook her head, like she was trying to shake off her past. "But everything's okay now. Rob is in jail and he's not coming out anytime soon. Not only did he threaten me at gunpoint, but he was also running for office and misusing the campaign funds."

"It was a terrible day, the day Rob Peterson came," Katie said. "But it was a proud one for us, too, because we stopped him."

"My dad hit him with one of my father-in-law's canes!" Anna exclaimed.

Melody could hardly believe the story she was hearing; it sounded so far-fetched—like something out of a storybook or on the movie screen. "And then Henry wanted to marry you?"

"Something like that." Anna's hands stilled as she continued to talk. "It's hard to explain, but somehow, while I was hiding out, I began to feel more comfortable here than at my own home. Things here mattered more to me. I told my parents I wanted to become Amish and then moved here and started learning as much as I could."

"I must say it was a slow process," Katie murmured as she approached Melody and took her sleeping baby from her arms. From what looked like nowhere, she pulled out a small wicker bassinet and placed Eli in it, securely wrapping the flannel blankets around him.

Then, seemingly satisfied, Katie went back to the story. "Anna didn't adjust all that easily."

"In some ways I did; in others, I didn't. For one thing, I missed watching television."

"I think she missed a lot of things," Katie added dryly. "You should have seen her try to can! She was a terrible Amish cook."

"Oh, stop. I wasn't that bad." Anna's eyes twinkled. "I wasn't that *gut*, though."

Winnie, who'd merely been smiling as Anna and Katie shared their story, chuckled. "She's still not that good."

Melody laughed. She liked these women, the way they worked easily together and the way they talked to each other. Full of teasing and fun. "The way you girls work together is wonderful-*gut*. It reminds me of how things are at my job."

Mrs. Brenneman nodded. "Work and chatter seem to bring out the best of us here. Where do you work?"

"In a coffeehouse."

"What do you do?"

"Wait on customers. I make baked goods, too. Cinnamon rolls, donuts, scones."

Mrs. Brenneman looked interested. "Scones? I've never made one of those."

"They're like biscuits. Most times, I put fruit in them. Any kind will do. Cranberries . . . blueberries."

"They sound delicious. If you weren't our guest, I'd ask you to make some."

"I'd love to, if you don't mind a guest puttering in your kitchen." Melody started to stand, eager to be of use. Eager to be invited into the women's close circle of friendship, if only for a little while . . .

"I wouldn't feel good about that, dear," Mrs. Brenneman said abruptly. "But I thank you just the same."

The refusal was kindly given. But the results were the same. And Melody still felt the sting. "Oh, of course," she said quickly, trying not to sound as awkward as she felt. "I mean, it was just an idea."

"And it was a good one," Katie agreed. "It's just that it's best if we don't let paying guests use the kitchen. You know how that goes. We'd never want something to happen to you."

Obviously, she was trying to take some of the sting out of her mother's refusal. And she did have a point. There were laws about keeping a kitchen clean and such. "Yes. Yes, of course."

"Besides, you had a long day of traveling. And you fainted! I don't know how you feel, but seeing you on the ground very well scared me half to death."

"I'm fine now, though."

"Perhaps, but it would be good for you to sit and relax,"

Mrs. Brenneman said. "We certainly don't want you to overdo things."

"The baby isn't due for three more weeks."

"*Jah*, but *bopplis* have a way of coming when they're ready," the older lady said sagely.

Katie looked over at her son, who was sleeping contentedly in his bassinet. "That's true. My Eli came on his own schedule."

"Was he early?"

Katie wrinkled her nose. "I wasn't that lucky. No, our boy came four days late."

"As most babies are," Mrs. Brenneman supplied. "Though my daughter here didn't want to hear about that."

"Not even a little bit." Anna chuckled. "Actually, Katie complained just about every hour of the day."

Katie arched a brow. "Just you wait until you are the one expecting, Anna. Then we'll see how patient you are."

"If I'm only half as impatient as you that will be saying a lot!"

Just hearing the women joke about labor and delivery made Melody's shoulders relax. Though she'd been too caught up with so much else, she had worried a bit about when the big day would come. It was a relief to know that it wasn't likely she would deliver anytime soon. "Well, chances are very good that I'll be back in Kentucky, bored and restless when it's my babe's time."

Katie looked at her more closely. "How is it you came to be here, Melody?"

"I took the bus."

"No, I mean, even coming here three weeks from your

due date is awfully close to your time. Actually, I'm surprised your family let you leave. How did you choose this inn, anyway?"

"My boss . . . she gave me a gift certificate."

"I'm thankful for that. But why did you decide now?"

Starting to feel uncomfortable, Melody stumbled over more words. "Well, after I deliver, I'll have a baby to watch over. I wouldn't be able to come here, then . . ."

"But for Christmas? Why don't you want to be home?"

"I . . . well . . ." Melody felt as if her throat was closing up.

Anna cleared her throat. "Melody, please forget Katie asked that." Turning to her sister-in-law, the blonde glared. "None of that is any of our business."

"I'm sorry. Am I being rude? I'm merely just curious. All I know is that my doctor said I needed to stay put when I was so close to my time. What did yours say? Do you have a doctor or are you going to use a midwife?"

"I have a doctor."

"Well, what did he say?"

"It's a woman . . ."

Katie put a hand on her hip and waited.

And waited.

Actually, all of them stared at her, wanting answers. And Melody couldn't really blame their curiosity, after all. Here Anna had just shared how she'd been held at gunpoint!

But Melody wasn't used to sharing. Nor was she used to talking about anything to do with the baby. As she struggled to tell them something, anything that wouldn't reduce her to tears, she could feel the blood leave her face. "I didn't ask my doctor's permission."

"What about your husband?"

Melody reached out to the counter for support as her world tilted. Oh, but she was afraid she was going to pass out again. "I don't have one."

All four women's eyes widened. Just as quickly, Katie closed them again. "Oh," she mumbled.

Just like her extended family in Kentucky, they were shocked.

Of course they were—her situation was shocking.

But carrying the burden alone for nine months was taking its toll. Melody's knees felt locked. She shook a foot slightly, hoping to regain some circulation. Anything to enable her to slink out of the room.

How had this happened? She'd gone from feeling happy to embarrassed in seconds. Now the room felt claustrophobic. Too hot. A wave of dizziness intensified, making her head spin.

As she gripped the counter, Melody chided herself again. Oh, but she should have known better. She should have made up a story. Told them her husband left her. Or he died. Something. Anything.

Anything other than her truth.

But she'd known that those lies wouldn't make her feel any better, and she would just be letting herself open to more prying questions. "I think I'll go lie down now."

Winnie trotted over and reached for her arm. "Wait, Melody. Please, don't go—"

"I—I must."

"Then I will walk you."

But just as Winnie was about to wrap a comforting arm around her shoulders, the situation became too much to bear. With a jerk, she avoided Winnie's hand and turned to the right. Quickly she raced down the hall. If she was quick enough, she could be in her room before the tears came. If she kept her mind on her steps, she would be in her room before she did something really stupid. Before she turned back around and told the women about getting attacked one evening on the way home from work.

Before she told them about how scared she'd been when the elderly couple found her, and then called the police.

How foreign the hospital had felt. How bruised and battered her body had been. How shamed she'd felt. For months.

As she climbed into the soft bed, the icy sheets caused her teeth to chatter. Soon enough she knew her body's heat combined with the down would warm her well and good. But at the moment she felt as cold as if she'd been exiled to the farthest reaches of the arctic.

Only far, far more alone.

The moment Melody disappeared, Anna glared at her. "Wow, Katie. Way to go."

"What?"

"You know what, daughter. Fact is, I am ashamed of you," her mother whispered. "Your prying questions were terribly rude. That girl's business is none of our concern."

Katie flinched. Oh, but she hated being admonished by her mother. "Mother, you know very well I didn't mean to make her cry. All I was doing was asking questions."

Winnie cleared her throat. "A whole lot of questions."

"I wasn't that bad."

Anna and Winnie exchanged glances. "Oh, I think you were," Winnie said.

But even as she tried to defend herself, Katie knew she wasn't quite being honest. She had grown up with guests in the house—Amish and English. They'd all come from different walks of life, too.

Some of the couples who came weren't married, and hadn't even pretended to be. Others did things she thought strange.

But early on, her parents had taught her not to judge. To maintain a comfortable camaraderie with everyone, yet to maintain an invisible wall between them and herself, especially with new guests. People who visited the bed-and-breakfast didn't necessarily come to make friends with the Brennemans. They came to relax.

And their inn was an *inn*, not a place to try to change people. Customers paid money to stay there. Money that was hard earned. They didn't deserve to be interrogated about their private lives . . . just as the Brennemans didn't care to be asked too many personal questions, either.

She knew that.

She also knew it wasn't her business how Melody had gotten in her condition, or if she was married or not. It certainly wasn't her place to judge. She should know that, too. Not too long ago, she'd been chased by regrets from her past, and had done an awful lot to keep those regrets from meeting the light of day.

But instead of holding true to those learnings, she'd acted on her own selfish desires. Every time she looked at Melody a little part of her brain informed her that it was time to face the truth—her erratic mood swings and tiredness had nothing to do with the busyness of the season.

It had far more to do with something else. The fact that she was pregnant again. The fact that she was trying to keep it a secret. The fact that she still hadn't told Jonathan and felt guilty about that.

Fearing that any defense of her rude behavior would only make matters worse, she held her tongue and hoped her mother would let things pass.

But obviously Anna could not. "How could Melody not have been offended?" she scolded, shaking her head in dismay. "Not only were your questions too personal, but your tone of voice was snippy, too."

"Snippy?"

"Oh, you know what I mean." Anna threw up her hands in dismay. "That poor thing came here, seeking refuge, and you've sent her to her room in shame."

Now her cheeks felt like they were on fire. "You're right, of course. I'll apologize to her later."

Anna rolled her eyes. "Oh, I'm sure that will make everything you said all better."

Katie's temper flared. "Stop acting so righteous. I was wrong, but you have to admit I wasn't asking questions out of thin air. Her situation is curious."

"Katie," her mother warned. "Again, I must caution that her life is none of our business."

"I know. But . . . what do you think happened?"

After checking to make sure no one was lurking outside the door, Winnie shrugged. "Probably the same thing that's happened to more women than we could count. She thought she was in love and rushed her wedding night. It happens and is unfortunate, but it's nothing to be shocked about."

"But why is she here?"

"Who knows?" Anna volunteered. "Maybe she just wanted a vacation."

"That's doubtful."

"Well, maybe she and her man are in a fight. Maybe her boyfriend will come looking for her on Christmas Day." Anna's eyes brightened. "Now that would be exciting, and so romantic, too."

Winnie sighed. "Terribly romantic."

Irene piped up. "The last thing I'm eager for is a commotion between two lovebirds on Christmas Day." After another moment passed, she said, almost reluctantly, "Something tells me that her situation isn't so rosy. What she needs is our kindness and prayer, yes?"

"*Jah.*" Holding Eli once again, Katie thought of everything that had happened to her over the last year. Just two years ago, she'd been a restless girl, sitting in this very kitchen, wishing something wonderful would happen to her. Wishing that Jonathan Lundy would one day finally notice her and come calling.

And call he did—but not in any way that she'd imagined. The widower had asked her to help care for his two daughters while his sister Winnie was in Indiana. After some discussion, her parents had reluctantly let her go. But it had been quite an adventure.

Jonathan's girls, Hannah and Mary, hadn't been all that accepting because they missed their mom. And she'd gotten some letters from a girl in her past.

Remembering just how topsy-turvy her life had felt, how out of control it had seemed to be, she wondered if her recent contentment had changed her. Had she now become the type of judgmental person she'd always claimed never to be? "I promise I really will apologize later," she said meekly. "I will try to become the friend she needs, too. I shouldn't have been so nosy. I don't know why I've been treating her so harshly."

"I don't know why you have, either," her mother said. "But it is time to stop. See that you do apologize, Katie."

In her arms, Eli's eyes drifted shut. Unable to stop herself, she gently pushed a stray lock of hair away from his forehead. "No matter what, I'm sure Melody will be as overcome as I was by her child's birth. Babies are miracles."

Even as she said the words, a flutter filled her stomach. Yes, babies were miracles. Even to new mothers who were already feeling overwhelmed.

Walking to her side, her mother pressed her lips to Katie's forehead. "Yes, indeed, they are. Now, however, we need to concentrate on the work to be done."

"Yes, let's make those cookies," Anna rushed to say. "My Henry will want something tasty to snack on this afternoon after being outdoors all day."

"'*My* Henry,'" Winnie mimicked with a smile.

"Oh, stop, Winnie," Anna said, her cheeks flaming. "You're just as dreamy when you speak of Sam."

"Perhaps," Winnie allowed.

"I just like to tease you because he's my brother," Katie said. "Never would I have ever imagined Henry being thought of that way."

"He's lucky I do. I'm a *gut frau*."

The three of them laughed as the tension dissipated and things were back to normal.

With a satisfactory smile, her mother nodded in Anna's direction and then walked over to the cupboard and pulled out a large bag of brown sugar. "I'm thinking molasses cookies might be just the thing," she murmured. "Let's get busy."

Chapter 7

December 21, 12:00 P.M.

Light rain started falling after two hours on the road. Soon after, the rain quickly turned to sleet, causing traffic to slow. Every lane was packed with cars, giant semis, smaller trucks, and an assortment of other vehicles. Some were loaded down with packages and gifts. Others were so filled with people that the drivers didn't seem to be paying too much attention to the road.

As the sleet continued to fall, people switched lanes without turn signals and seemed eager to blow their horns for the slightest infraction. It was stressful.

So stressful, that Leah had to do anything she could to remain calm and in control. She listened to music, all the while imagining the look of surprise that was sure to appear on Melody's face when she showed up at the Brenneman Bed and Breakfast out of the blue.

No doubt, her girlfriend would start crying within minutes, too. She was a crier.

Actually, Melody was kind of everything. From the minute Leah had met her Amish friend, she'd been struck by the way Melody had yet to meet an emotion that she didn't wear on her sleeve. She was such a sweetheart. Leah was so glad she'd decided to ask for a few days off to visit her.

No one should be alone so close to Christmas.

Just as Leah was driving under a bridge on the interstate, and was carefully navigating the lanes as the traffic changed from three lanes to two, construction zone signs appeared. She frowned as she gripped the wheel tightly. The already crowded lanes narrowed as the road dipped into a valley. Combined with the driving rain and sleet, it took all her concentration to stay in her lane and keep with the traffic flow.

Sweat beaded her brow as she came upon a line of concrete-filled orange barrels. Now the lanes felt claustrophobic. There was nowhere to go except forward. At regular intervals, she looked to her left and right, making sure she was aware of where the rest of the cars were at all times.

Then the cars in front of her screeched to a halt. She slammed on her brakes.

Around her, cars swerved and then perilously slid on the already slick pavement. Metal crashed into metal, horns blared, people yelled, and airbags flew open.

Leah gripped her steering wheel hard as she could as she tried her best to not only get out of the way of careening cars, but to escape hitting the Toyota in front of her head-on. As she felt the vibrations of the antilocks doing their best, panic rose in her. She had no control over her vehicle. No way of stopping. "Please, God," she whispered. "Please—"

Her body reverberated against the seat belt as her Civic met the inevitable. Luckily, it wasn't quite hard enough to send the air bag out, but the impact was jarring.

She was shaking now. Shaking. Crying. "Please God. Please God."

All around her, a dozen cars fell into the same situation. Each slammed or rolled into another vehicle, or the median. Or the shoulder. Or the railing. One right after the other with enough force to push a long line of vehicles smack dab into one another—just like a row of cards or dominoes.

Leah was thankful that the jolt she'd received hadn't done too much more than bruise her slightly and leave her emotionally shaken. She was sure others hadn't been near as lucky.

While she was still in an adrenaline rush, she coaxed her car to the shoulder of the highway. There was really no way anyone could get around her at the moment, but she felt safer with her car off to the side.

For a split second, she praised God for being by her side—and praised Mr. Johnson, her ancient driving instructor. He'd been the one who had made her practice what to do in emergencies in the driving simulator.

After putting her Civic in Park, and pretty much resigning herself that the car was never going to shift into Drive again, she lifted up her emergency brake, just to be on the safe side. Finally, she breathed a sigh of relief and looked around.

The highway looked like a parking lot.

Now she was just high enough on the crest of the hill to understand what had begun all this mess. About a mile up ahead, two semis had collided. One was halfway off the road. Only one lane was open, and it was being used by emergency vehicles.

There was no way Leah was going to be going anywhere for hours. Her little Honda's front bumper was smashed, and the backend was damaged enough to put it out of commission forever.

She couldn't catch her breath. Tears fell in spurts as she tried to get her bearings. She was okay.

Leah wasn't sure how long she sat there. Five minutes? Twenty? She felt as if she was looking through the rest of the highway in a daze. As if she was just an observer.

Like the scene around her was in a movie she was watching.

Slowly, she unbuckled. Since a few people had gotten out of their cars, she decided to do the same. With her heart racing, she unlocked her door, and satisfied that other drivers around her were doing the same thing, she got out.

Immediately, Leah regretted that action. The temperature was bitterly cold and the rain and sleet mixture felt brutal against her cheeks. Obviously, it was just a hint of

things to come. Too late, she remembered that the fore-
casters had predicted more snow and cold in Louisville.
Wind gusted and ice shards stung her face—a hint of
things to come in Ohio, where likely a huge cold front
was already moving in. She had hoped to make it to the
inn before the weather turned bad, but there sure wasn't
a chance of that now.

She'd just slipped on her hat and gloves and was wondering who to call—911? AAA?—and had decided to take
a closer look at her car's front end when a very handsome
patrolman made his way over.

"You should stay in your vehicle, ma'am. It's safer for
you inside than out here. Warmer, too."

Since her nose felt numb, she had to agree. But Leah still
couldn't resist teasing him a bit. "Safer from the weather
or from other cars?"

He looked around at the long line of fender benders and
scowling people. "Both," he said dryly. "These types of
things bring out the worst in people. And it is really cold."

The officer was tall. At least six foot. He had the kind
of jaw and cheekbones that looked carved out of stone.
But he didn't look hard. No, his eyes were kind. And his
demeanor was relaxed and easy. Even the cold didn't seem
to affect him all that much.

She lifted her cell phone. "I've never been in an accident
like this before. I'm not sure what to do."

"We've got some tow trucks on the way. Yours is one
of the ones that's going to need a lift, I'm afraid." With a
frown, he tapped the Civic's smashed back end. "It's not
going anywhere."

"I think you're right."

"Hello? Officer?" Behind them, an elderly man was calling for assistance.

The patrolman turned the man's way and grimaced. "He's in bad shape. Listen, I've got to go help him."

"I understand."

He stepped away, but looked reluctant to do so. "More officers are coming, but they're having a hard time getting here, what with all the accidents."

"Okay." Why was he telling her so much?

His eyes met hers. "What I'm trying to say is, why don't you hop back in your Civic and stay put until I come back? Then I'll help you."

He would? That sounded awfully nice. And too good to be true. "You think you're going to have time to come back my way?"

"Of course. It's what I'm here for."

As his calm words registered, her muscles relaxed. Maybe she was going to get out of this mess in one piece and then figure out how to get to the inn.

For a moment, he looked like he was going to touch her arm, but he didn't. However, his voice did gentle. "I promise, miss. I'll come back and help you. But in the meantime, I don't want you to freeze. Go sit in your car, turn on the engine and get warm if you can, and I'll be back soon." He turned and started trotting to the man.

Impulsively, Leah called out, "Officer, be careful!"

Looking her way over his shoulder, he winked. "Always."

Bemused, Leah followed his directions. She got in her

car, turned the engine back on, leaned against the seat cushion—and watched.

He patiently listened to the elderly man who'd been calling out to him, nodded to another, and patted a woman's arm. He sure did seem extremely capable.

Then, of course, she couldn't help but smile at herself. What in the world had just happened? Was she really sitting in her car, admiring a highway patrolman?

Uh, yes.

There was something special about him. She felt an unexplainable connection with him that she'd never felt before. Of course, that was really crazy. Right?

Twenty minutes later, he returned. Quickly, she rolled down her window. "You're back," she said.

"I promised I would be." When he bent down to talk to her through the opening, she realized that his eyes were light brown. Almost amber or citrine in color. Almost golden.

"So, are you still okay?"

"I'm fine. Well, as good as I can be, stuck on the freeway," she amended.

"Good." He smiled encouragingly. "Just over the bend, four tow trucks are on the way."

Unfortunately, there were at least six cars surrounding her that looked like they needed to be towed. "It's going to take a bunch more than four to get this cleaned up."

"Oh, yeah. It's a nightmare." But instead of looking perturbed, he grinned. "Don't worry. I've seen worse."

As a horn blared in the background, the officer rolled his eyes. "Everyone is getting impatient."

She felt bad for monopolizing him. "Listen, you don't have to keep coming back to check on me."

"I want to. It's just, well . . . is there any way you'd be able to wait a bit to get rescued?"

"Huh?"

His cheeks flushed. "There's some folks in a Cadillac a couple of cars over who need assistance, and a woman who's six months' pregnant who I'd like to get to shelter as soon as possible, too." Searching her face, he said, "I'm sure you've got things to do, but—"

She cut him off. "I'm healthy and not in that big of a hurry. I can wait."

"You're sure?"

"Of course, Officer. I can wait my turn."

His eyes positively lit up. "I can't tell how glad I am to hear that. Okay. Here's the deal, I'm going to work with the other officers to get the worst cases cleared away ASAP."

"And then?"

"And then I'll be back shortly with an update."

The way he looked at her, like Leah actually mattered to him, gave her a little jolt of pleasure. For the last year, all she'd done was go to class, study, and work. She hadn't had time to date. Certainly no time to start a relationship.

But this man appealed to her. And once more, what was happening between them seemed to be out of her hands—just like the accident. Like it was inevitable.

Slowly, she ventured, "You'll come back, or will it be someone else?"

"Me."

"I'm glad."

White teeth flashed. "I told the other guys that you were all mine." A look of horror crossed his face. "Oh. Excuse me. I mean, scratch that. I mean, we're all trying to connect with one or two people out here so y'all aren't hearing conflicting reports."

"It's fine. Go to work." She looked at his nametag. "Officer Littleton."

"Just for the record, miss—it's Zack."

"I'm Leah."

He tapped her door with two fingers. "Leah . . . stay here and be safe. I promise, I'll be back as soon as I can."

"I'll be waiting," she murmured after she rolled up her window and watched him once again try to calm some other accident victims down.

Now she was sitting in her injured vehicle while tow trucks were being summoned and AAA was working with her to get a rental car.

Things being what they were—and the fact that at least eight other cars were in the same position, and given that there was a steady stream of ambulances and fire trucks and police cars around—Leah knew it was time to grab a hotel for the night. In Louisville.

She was scared. She'd never gotten a hotel room by herself before. Plus, Louisville was a big city. She had no idea even where to find a hotel, let alone one that was in a safe part of town. She'd grown up hearing plenty of stories about bad things that happened to foolish vacationers in Louisville or Cincinnati.

Realizing that she was letting her imagination get the best of her, Leah forced herself to calm down. And then she realized she really was being pretty silly. Just being in a big city didn't mean she was in danger . . .

Melody was proof enough that bad things could happen anywhere, at any time.

Since she had plenty of time to wait, she called her mom and gave her an update. Her mom, of course, had offered to drive out and get her. But Leah knew if she went home and actually had time to think about making the drive—well, she wouldn't be going anywhere.

Her well-intentioned visit to Melody would be just that—a good intention that never went anywhere.

So, she'd done her best to sound braver than she felt. And tried to act calmer than she was with the police officer who kept coming back to check on her.

Zack, his name was. And as far as she was concerned, he was one of God's angels. He'd been so kind to her, so helpful, she knew that couldn't have been in his job description.

As if just thinking about him had conjured him up again, he rapped on her window. "Miss? Leah?"

She opened her door and got out. "Yes?"

"You didn't have to get out again." He smiled, revealing one tooth that was slightly crooked. "I was just checking up on you."

"I'm fine. But thank you, sir."

"It's Zack, remember?"

"Of course," she replied with a smile.

As around her, emergency vehicles continued to load injured people and other cars slowly moved past on the far-left lane, he leaned up against the side of her car and crossed his arms over his chest. Just like he was watching a soccer game or something.

With effort, she tried to mimic his posture, hoping to look nonchalant, too. But it was hard. Inside, she was still as nervous as could be. And her body was starting to feel the effects of the crash. "Is it okay that you're standing here with me again?"

"Of course. You were in an accident, right?" He nodded his head slightly, signaling her to agree.

"Ah, yes?"

"My job is to assist everyone and anyone I can. You count."

His comment spurred a laugh. "Thanks for that. I've been so stressed, I didn't think I could laugh."

"The Lord makes sure there's no journey we can't handle."

His statement brought her up short. "You're a Christian?"

"You bet. You can't have this job and not be. Well, that's my opinion. We all need miracles and the Grace of God on a daily basis."

What a strange conversation they were having. Never would she have believed it was possible to be talking about faith and car accidents all at the same time.

But here they were.

His words made her feel a thousand times better. With Zack standing by her side, waiting on the side of the road didn't seem all that bad. "I'm glad you're here."

Something sweet and genuine flickered in his eyes. "I

hope you don't find this weird, but I'm glad you're here, too."

To Leah's surprise, she suddenly hoped that her tow truck was going to be stuck in traffic for at least a little while longer.

Chapter 8

December 21, 2:00 P.M.

Levi knew the Brenneman Bed and Breakfast was only two miles from State Highway 32, as the crow flies. The driver he'd hired had had no trouble locating the inn, or getting to it fairly quickly—which Levi's wallet had been thankful for. So he knew that it was fairly close to the city.

But from where he was standing now, surrounded by clusters of shrubs and trees with snow-glistening leaves and limbs, they might have been in the thick of the wilderness. No cars could be heard rumbling near the entrance of the Brenneman property. No echo of semis and trucks could be detected from the interstate.

All that could be heard—outside of Hannah Lundy's laughter in the barn—were the faint cries of birds as they darted back and forth through the trees. Those trees had held his interest for some time as he glanced around, noting with appreciation the size of the age-old oaks as well as the peaceful hush created by the layered skirtlike limbs of the pine trees. He didn't live on a farm, and his work schedule was such that he had little spare time for long walks or hikes.

And his mind, of course, had been unable to do anything but grieve.

But now, as his head cleared and the opportunity arose, he found himself looking forward to being outdoors for a change. He was also eager for the day's activity. A hunt.

"I could have sworn we were just going to chop wood," he said when Henry Brenneman came close.

"We were, but then my *daed* had a better idea." He grinned slowly. "I'd rather track a deer than chop wood any day of the week."

"I'll side with you. I've never hunted before, but I have chopped my share of wood."

As they continued to wait for the other men to join them, Henry looked Levi over. "I'm glad you're wearing layers. It gets warm out here."

" 'Warm' is a relative thing, *jah*? It's near fifteen degrees."

"Yes, but we don't hunt like old people. No strolling among the brambles for us." He pushed his shoulders back a bit. "We men like to carry on at a good clip."

Again, Levi felt himself grinning. He'd missed this— the banter of masculine bravado, found only in the company of other men his own age. It reminded him that he was still young, hardy and alive.

Thirty minutes later, Levi reckoned Henry's "good clip" had been a little bit of an understatement. Henry, Jonathan, Mr. Brenneman all walked like they were being timed. Levi was used to hard work, but not so much walking briskly in thick boots. He found himself pausing to catch his breath every few feet.

"Is this too much for ya?" Mr. Brenneman called out. "We can take a breather, if you'd like."

There was no way on earth Levi was going to look at a man old enough to be his father and admit that he couldn't keep up with him! "I'll be fine."

Though Henry and Jonathan had marched on, limberly hopping over a fallen tree and veering right, the older man paused for him. "No shame in admitting your faults, Levi."

"I'm not afraid to admit mine. But walking in the woods ain't one of them."

Mr. Brenneman chuckled. "All right, then," he said, then turned and somehow managed to walk even faster. Snow crunched underfoot as he practically marched along.

In spite of his best efforts, Levi found himself breathing harder. "Jesus, I know you're laughing at me," Levi murmured. "I have a hunch that you're warning me to speak up, to admit my physical faults. I know my pride is getting in the way."

But instead of asking Mr. Brenneman to slow his pace, Levi compensated by unbuttoning his wool coat. When he did, the cool air refreshed him and he followed the men— they were about twenty yards up ahead, talking about a horse auction.

Satisfied he hadn't lost them, Levi slowed for a moment

and gazed at the beauty that surrounded him. Truly, the area was a sight to see. The Brennemans' land was hilly and filled to the brim with nature's glory. Tall oaks stood company with maples and ash trees. A sprinkling of pine kept the area green even now, in the dead of winter.

In the far distance was a large pasture—the ground brown and bare, dormant. Beyond that lay the outline of a barn and a group of dairy cows.

"You coming, Levi?"

"I am," he called back. To his embarrassment, his words sounded strained. Even to his own ears.

Picking up his pace again, he followed the other men through a maze of trees. Then stopped next to them near an outcropping of rocks.

Jonathan studied him as he finally approached. "Glad you could make it," he teased.

"I've been finding it hard to race through the woods," he retorted. "You all are walking kind of fast, don'tcha think?"

"Not so fast."

"I'm just sayin' that it's kind of hard to see deer that way."

Henry slapped him on the back. "We're going to slow down now. We were just trying to get away from the house. Ain't safe to hunt so close."

They'd been walking a good forty-five minutes, and resting for ten. At last his breathing was starting to return to normal. "Do you all plan to continue going for a while yet?" Levi hoped he didn't sound too hopeful.

Mr. Brenneman answered. *"Nee."*

Henry laughed. "It's true. Keep your eyes peeled, Levi. Any and all bucks are now fair game for Christmas dinner."

Jonathan pulled out a thermos of coffee from the knapsack on his back and sipped. "Care for any?"

Gratefully, Levi sipped the hot liquid. *"Danke."*

Once the other men had taken a fortifying sip, they all started walking again. This time at a slower pace. Levi was thankful. He took the opportunity to again study the beautiful surroundings.

About five minutes later, Mr. Brenneman looked his way. "I'm guessin' you don't live near the woods up in Berlin?"

"Not at all. I live on a street with several other houses."

"And what is it you do there?"

"I work at a garage-door factory."

Henry looked at him with interest. "Is it an Amish-owned enterprise?"

"Nee. Mennonite. It's a good job. The hours are good and the pay is fair."

"That's all a man can ask for," Jonathan murmured. "And your boss, is he a good man?"

"He is at that. The owners are caring, Christian men. They were good to me"—he caught himself before he talked of how kind Kevin, his boss, had been when Rosanna passed on—"over the years."

If the other men noticed his clumsy wording, no one looked like he cared. "That is a blessing. I work in a lumberyard," Jonathan said. "My boss is an *Englischer.* We get along well."

Levi was surprised. He'd assumed all three men either worked at the inn or farmed. "Working at a job, with other men, is a good thing, I think."

Henry nodded wearily. "There's many a day I would

gladly change places with Jonathan. Working side by side with my wife and parents ain't always rosy."

"Why do you say that?" his father asked.

Henry's eyes widened in alarm, then he laughed sheepishly when he spied the humor in his dad's face. "No reason. It's also nice, of course."

"I don't know how I'd feel, doing anything else. I'm happy where I am," Levi stated. My boss is agreeable and pays a fair wage. That's good enough for me."

"Brent, my boss, helped us out when my barn burned down," Jonathan said quietly. "He donated a lot of the wood, and let me buy the rest of it at cost. He even came to the barn raising."

"Good bosses like that are hard to find," Levi agreed. For a moment, he was tempted to go ahead and share how Kevin had not only given him paid days off, but had taken up a collection for Levi to help pay for his wife's hospital bills.

Of course, he didn't mention that, though. Discussing anything to do with Rosanna's death would ruin the entire reason he'd left Berlin.

"It's cold, but at least it's not snowing . . . ain't so?" he blurted. The comment obviously came out of nowhere, but perhaps the men wouldn't mind.

With a perceptive glance, Henry nodded. "Clear skies are always more welcome than snowy ones," he agreed. "Of course, we weren't as lucky last year."

Mr. Brenneman took up the wayward tangent next. With a gruff chuckle, he began to tell a long, convoluted tale about the men's hunting trip the previous year.

wasn't Amish until recently. Until then, her chicken was wrapped in plastic and frozen at the grocery store," responded Henry.

"And she'd never eaten deer—she said the animals were too pretty to eat," added Jonathan.

"I'm afraid I'm not much more of a hunter than Anna is. But I'm willing to learn. How do you intend to get this animal back home?"

"First we must dress it here," John Brenneman said, taking a knife out of a worn leather scabbard. "We'll remove what we won't use, bury it, and then prepare to carry our prize home."

Jonathan whistled low. "To carefully carry it home."

Levi pretended his stomach didn't turn somersaults as John carefully made an incision along the deer's belly and then proceeded to gut the poor animal.

But he didn't think the other men were fooled for one second. It was a difficult thing, to take another animal's life. But it was also the way of the world. The deer meat would not be wasted. And the time they spent hunting and preparing it for eating wouldn't be forgotten, either.

Henry slapped him on the back. "You doing all right, there, Levi? You're looking a bit green."

"I am." He smiled weakly. "It's quite a sight, though. I'm afraid I'm almost as squeamish as a girl."

"Not quite. My Anna would be in tears by now, I'll tell you that. If she had her way, we'd have a salt lick outside for the deer and she'd be giving them names. She's right fond of them."

"It's *gut* she didn't go with us, then."

"You have no idea." Henry looked over and smiled. "My *daed* has our deer ready now. Let's cart this beast home and show the women, *jah*?"

"I'll be glad to help carry it."

Thankful that he wore gloves, Levi stood where Henry placed him and helped pick up the animal after they carefully wrapped a tarp around it.

The deer was a good size—at least two hundred pounds. But between the four of them its weight wasn't unbearable. On Sam's count of three, they hefted the animal and started toward home.

The cold temperatures helped with the bleeding, but being what it was, blood on their clothes couldn't be helped. "We're making a real mess of you, Levi."

"It's true. I hope there's a place I can do laundry."

"Don't be silly. If the women are washing our shirts and pants, they can wash yours, too. After all, the mess is for a good cause, yes?"

Grinning, Levi nodded. Though he wasn't sure if he was a fan of hunting, he was enjoying the exercise and companionship. And the realization that he hadn't thought of Rosanna in almost three hours.

December 21, 5:00 P.M.

"The men are back," the littlest of the two girls—Hannah, Melody thought she was named—called out. "They're back and they've brought us home a deer!"

As Melody heard the multiple exclamations and watched

members of the family go racing outside, she retreated to the back of the entryway. From there it was easy to view things and, surprisingly, too, easy to blend in with the surroundings. People walked by with intent to get somewhere, and seemed to only imagine she was busy, too.

Melody almost felt herself smiling as she spied the hunters' proud expressions. Oh, but they looked full of themselves, like they'd just saved the area from the fearful threat of a wayward buck!

Almost as comical were the expressions of their womenfolk. Mrs. Brenneman, especially, seemed to be wavering between excitement and exasperation—of both having fresh venison for Christmas dinner and the experience to know of the enormous amount of work that was going to take place in order to store the deer meat for the winter.

Melody was just wondering where to go next when Levi entered, his cheeks ruddy from the cold.

As soon as he saw her, he hesitated. "You ought to come out and see our prize. It's quite a sight."

She hugged her stomach. "Oh, I don't think so. I feel queasy enough these days without looking at a dead animal."

To her surprise, instead of looking uncomfortable at the mention of her pregnancy, he chuckled. "I know what you mean. Rosanna had a terrible time with some smells. Why, it didn't matter whether an egg was boiled or fried, she could hardly stand the sight of it."

Melody didn't know who Rosanna was, but he was so touchy about his personal life, she didn't dare ask. "Eggs haven't bothered me none. Only raw meat. But did you enjoy yourself?"

"You know what? I did. We hiked quite a bit, it was *gut* exercise. It's chilly out, though. I hope they have some coffee here."

"I just saw Anna put out some fresh cookies and coffee on the sideboard in the dining room."

His eyes lit up. "As soon as I clean up, that's where I'm headed." He paused. "In twenty minutes or so, once I've gotten fit for company again . . . would you care to join me?"

"You wouldn't mind?" She didn't know if she was more surprised by his offer or her willingness to accept it.

"I wouldn't mind at all. As a matter of fact, I would welcome your company."

As she stood there next to him, she became suddenly very aware of his gaze. Of his shy, reticent manner. Melody felt another startling pull toward him. "Then I will save you a seat in the living room."

"I won't be long," he promised, then left her to climb the stairs. Melody hugged herself as she settled in one of the big comfortable chairs to await him.

A curious fluttering filled her stomach. For a moment, she worried it was the baby. It was with some surprise when she realized what that fluttering was . . .

Eager anticipation. Yes. She was eagerly anticipating Levi's return to the room. In a way she'd anticipated no other man's presence in a very long time.

Chapter 9

December 21, 11:45 P.M.

Melody was trapped. The man's hands were crushing as he held her down. As he covered her mouth with his own. His breath was rank, his teeth bit at her lips when she tried to scream.

He tilted his head, moved his hand over her throat. Cutting off her airway. She couldn't breathe.

Little by little, the pain of her body subsided as her brain concentrated on breathing. But, like the rest of her body, her lungs were losing the battle. They contracted, her brain fogged.

It was inevitable. She was going to die.

With that realization came an overwhelming sense of

calm. No longer did she try to fight. No longer did she worry about the pain. Or what would happen to her.

Soon, she would be in God's hands. He would care for her, just as He cared for all of His lambs. As she stopped struggling for air, the burning in her lungs lessened. Soon, visions of green hills and pastures flooded her brain. A sense of peace calmed her. No longer would she have to fear rejection. No longer would she be alone.

No, she'd be with her Father. He would comfort her . . .

Little by little, the cement under her back didn't feel so hard and cold. The smell of the stale beer on her assailant's breath faded. The pain ripping through her body no longer was overwhelming. Soon, it wouldn't matter anymore.

And then she woke up.

Gripping her sheets like a lifeline, Melody gasped— breathing as deep as she could, sucking in a breath. In response, her lungs burned, filling with air awkwardly. A cold, harsh sweat formed on her brow as she struggled to sit up.

As she did, Melody welcomed the cool, fresh air into her lungs. Air meant she was okay. The biting temperature reminded her that it was not summer, it was December. She was far from the street where she'd been grabbed.

No one was in the room but her. She was alone.

Again, Melody inhaled quickly, then inhaled again, forcing herself to breathe in and breathe out. Steadily.

Just like she'd learned from the social worker.

Little by little, reality returned. She was not in Sonora. She was in Adams County, Ohio. At the Brenneman Bed and Breakfast. She was not alone on the side of the road.

She was in a beautiful guest bedroom. Her door had a lock on it.

And, best of all, she could breathe.

With shaking hands, Melody pulled the thick layers of covers back and pulled at the neckline of her nightgown. Finally unfastened the very top button. The new inch of room allowed her to move her head and shoulders. She exhaled in relief.

It had been this way almost every night since she'd been violated. The nurses at the hospital and the counselors at the care center had assured her that such nightmares were normal. That while her body was healing, her brain had to heal, too, and sometimes the only way to do that was to relive the incident, because during the day, when she was awake, she pushed it away.

It hurt too much to talk about.

Her nightgown and sheets were damp from perspiration. Oh, but those bad dreams caused her body to shake and shiver. With effort, she got to her feet and walked across the room to her robe and wrapped it around her. However, cold snatches of air whispered through the gap in the fabric. Her girth had made the robe too small.

After searching in her suitcase, she pulled out a pair of wool socks her sister had knitted for her last Christmas. Awkwardly, she lifted her foot and twisted in order to pull them on.

She was large now. So heavy and big with child. With her attacker's child. With Mark Gillman's child.

No one else knew his name. She'd asked the policemen to keep his name from her family. What she was going through was hard enough without anyone else having a name to focus on. To her great relief, the authorities had succumbed to her wish. Rape cases were treated as confidentially as possible, she'd learned.

One lady detective told her that she'd personally had done her best to keep Melody's name from ever being spoken aloud.

"You're already a victim," she'd said softly. "No way are you going to be maligned any further."

To Melody's surprise, the lady detective had kept her word.

Now, Mark Gillman was in jail. For at least eight years, she was told.

Oh, not from raping her, but because he had raped and robbed another woman just two days after he'd attacked her. Unlike Melody, that woman had fought hard. So hard that she'd barely survived the beating. She'd also been vocal about her attack, had gotten a lawyer, and had testified in court.

It was because of that woman that justice had been served. That woman's bravery had landed that man in jail. Not Melody's.

Her parents had celebrated the news; justice had been served. Melody, however, had no further involvement. After all, she hadn't had to compromise her Amish beliefs—as her family had reminded her, it was the Lord's place to avenge her attacker, not hers. Knowing they were trying to be helpful, she had listened to them.

Of course, they had also been attempting to shoo away the incident as well.

Perhaps that had been the right decision. However . . . sometimes, in the middle of the night, she wasn't so sure. All she knew was that the nights when she wasn't consumed with reliving the horror and the past, her dreams turned fretful with worries about the baby and the future.

And in her present physical state . . . well, there was mostly discomfort. Just weeks ago, she did her best to ignore her body's struggle to make room for the growing baby. But, of course, that was hardly possible any longer. The baby had dropped some and was likely to be born within the next three weeks. And then, once again, her life would be changed dramatically. For better? For worse? Oh, how she wished she knew the answer!

The rocking chair made barely a creak as she gingerly moved back and forth. She tried to keep her eyes from straying to the clock, couldn't help herself. Midnight! That was bad news. She was wide awake.

From experience, she knew she would now be facing lonely hours, sitting in the dark with only disturbing thoughts for company. On impulse, she moved the shade to one side, but it was a futile gesture. Nothing could be seen in the blackness.

Perhaps coming to the inn had been a worse idea than she'd imagined. So far, she hadn't found the solace she'd been looking for. Though Katie now seemed welcoming instead of resentful of her presence, it hardly helped—neither did the Brennemans' curious looks.

Or Levi Bender's scowl. Oh, that man. He was by turns grumpy or almost friendly. They'd shared cookies together, but then later he looked so ill at ease he acted like he didn't even want to be in the same room with her.

Wouldn't he be surprised to know that she didn't blame him for his feelings at all? She, too, was at a loss. She felt embarrassed and worried and scared.

And so completely, totally worthless.

Tears welled up in her eyes again. And though she hated the weakness, Melody gave in and let the tears fall. The emotion wracking her body. Filling her soul.

Making her gasp for air again.

December 22, midnight

Standing at the side of their bed, Katie Lundy tugged at her husband's shoulder. "Jonathan, she's crying again."

Slow as molasses, he opened one eye. "Who?" Before she could answer, he closed his eye again and drifted back to sleep.

Katie patted his shoulder again. "Who do you think? Melody, that's who. Wake up and talk to me."

With a sigh, he pulled one arm out from under a thick down-filled comforter. Reached for her. "I think not. It's pitch black outside. Come to bed, Katie."

She pulled her hand away. "I can't." As he turned to his side, Katie pushed back her hair over one shoulder and turned to the door. The dull beat of anguished tears floated through the door. Each sound was filled with such pain, it nearly broke her heart. "She sounds really upset, Jonathan. I hope she's okay."

Watching her for another moment, her husband slowly sat up, rubbing his eyes. "What time is it?"

"Late."

"How late?"

"After midnight." Now that she had his attention, she turned away from the door and sat on the edge of the bed. Though she usually loved falling asleep in his comforting embrace, Katie knew she wasn't anywhere close to relaxing.

"And you've been up all evening?"

"Yes. I started working on my quilt and lost track of time."

"But you were so tired earlier. You acted like you couldn't wait to crawl into bed."

"I know, it makes no sense to me," she murmured, though actually she had a very good feeling about what was wrong with her. "It's like I have no control over my body and emotions right now. Sometimes I cry for no reason, other times I feel so full of joy, I hardly can contain myself."

"It doesna make much sense. Do you think you're sick?"

"No . . . I think this is just a passing thing. Soon I'll feel right as rain."

He looked her over, slowly, like he was examining every inch of her. "You said the coffee didn't agree with you the other morning."

"I know, but today it tasted just as good as ever." She looked away, not wanting to meet his searching gaze. "Perhaps I had a cold."

"But now?"

"Now?" She fidgeted. "I feel just fine."

"These symptoms are worrying me."

He did look worried, and suspicious, too. Katie felt a lump in her throat. He, too, was most likely recalling all the changes her body had gone through with Eli. She knew she should tell him that she thought she was pregnant.

But she just wasn't quite ready.

So she pushed things off again. "Oh, I hope not. Please don't worry, Jonathan. All that's kept me up this evening has been my quilting." She pulled it out of the basket where she'd tossed it earlier and held it up for him to see. "What do you think?"

He chuckled. "I think it's a pretty thing, to be sure. But you're going to lose your eyesight, stitching with only this lamp next to you."

"It's a Christmas present for Mary. It must get done." Carefully, she smoothed the pretty red-and-green star quilt over her lap. She knew her daughter was going to love the festive colors.

"What you must do is sleep," he chided gently. "Eli wakes up early, you know. He won't care if his mother has been working on something for his sister. He'll only care about wanting your attention."

"You're right. Eli will be eager for me—at least his stomach, *jah*?" Even hearing his name made her smile. Yes, her baby was a wonderful-*gut* addition to her life. In her opinion, he made their family complete. She loved Jonathan's Mary and Hannah like her own, and loved her husband with her whole heart. But there had been a small portion of her being that had wanted a baby of her own. She'd enjoyed her pregnancy as much as possible—and now looked, with Eli by her side, with wonder at all the world. He was a happy baby, easy-going and agreeable.

She had so very much to praise God for.

But she couldn't help but contrast her good fortune with Melody. She no longer heard the woman's cries, but that didn't ease Katie's conscience. She herself had spent a night or two in tears, muffling her sounds so no one else would hear her. "Jonathan, I feel so sorry for our guest."

"I know. But her problems aren't ours, Katie."

"Now I feel so terrible . . . for ever resenting her staying here."

"It wasn't a personal thing," he said lightly. "I'm sure she would understand that."

"But still, it was wrong of me. I had a plan in my head and it was getting changed. You know how that makes me feel."

"Irritated." He pulled the covers back. "Now, will you turn off the lamp and join me?"

After carefully folding the Christmas quilt and hiding it in a drawer, she turned off the lamp and crawled into bed. Instead of feeling icy cold sheets, the bed was warm and inviting, thanks to her husband's presence.

As he wrapped his arms around her, she whispered, "How do you think I can help Melody?"

"I don't know. If she's been crying a lot, she has more problems than we might ever be able to solve." He paused, letting Katie know that he was still thinking. "Perhaps you could talk to her about Eli? About your experiences with labor and delivery and caring for a newborn? The only thing we do know is that she will soon be holding her own baby in her arms."

"That is *gut* advice, husband." She had been anxious about the unknown.

"I am full of good advice," he teased. "Such as, we need to stop talking and go to sleep."

She snuggled closer and let her eyes drift shut. There, in the bedroom she grew up in, her life was full and joyous. She had so much to be grateful for.

Why had she worried so much about a stranger taking her joy? As her husband's deep breaths turned into gentle snores, she promised herself to reach out to their guest some more.

After all, she was so blessed, it was the least she could do.

Chapter 10

December 22, 8:00 A.M.

It had taken almost twenty-four hours to get a rental car. But just as soon as Leah had received the vehicle and signed the papers, the second half of the storm arrived. Fresh snow and an ice storm pummeled the area, causing yet another stream of accidents on I-71.

She knew because Zack had asked her out for breakfast at the hotel restaurant and told her all about the traffic reports. "Of course, it's up to you," he said, his expression earnest. "But if you can spare the time at all, I'd suggest you stay another day, just to be on the safe side."

Leah's stomach clenched at even the thought of waiting another two hours. "The accidents are really that bad?"

"Everyone who's reported in said there are cars spinning

off the road left and right. And, well, there're parts of the corridor from Louisville to Cincinnati that are notoriously bad. Every time there's ice, we can bank on accidents. I would hate for anything to happen to you." After meeting her gaze for a moment, he looked back at his plate, suddenly shy. "Of course, it's your call. I'm just sayin' . . ."

"That me and my rental car might have a time of it," Leah finished with a smile.

Of course, she couldn't help but smile at a lot of things about Officer Zack Littleton. First of all, he was flatout handsome. Today, he wore jeans, a flannel shirt, and Timberlands. He looked more his age and less imposing than in his uniform.

The light of day also illuminated his square jaw and hazel-colored eyes. And his dark blond hair. He really was cute.

Leah knew she should have been cursing her luck, and be out of sorts. She knew she should be feeling more frustrated than ever. After all, so far nothing had gone right on the trip. But even though she did feel some of that, she also was feeling a little bit lucky.

Something about Zack felt right. Really right.

"Do you do this often?" she blurted. "Do you have breakfast with people you meet while working?"

He looked horrified. "Never."

"Then, why me?" She hated to be so forward, but she wanted to know.

To her amazement, a faint sheen of red stained his cheeks. "Because I think you're pretty," he mumbled. "And because I thought you were easy to talk to. And . . . I don't know. I thought there was something that clicked between us." He closed his eyes for a second. "Wow. I sound really cheesy." Tossing his paper napkin on the table, he looked ready to bolt. "Would you like me to leave? Am I making you uncomfortable?"

To her surprise, his awkwardness made her feel even more at ease. "No. I mean, no, you don't. And thank you for the compliment."

"Is it a compliment if it's true? You are really pretty. Nice, too."

"Thank you. I think you're nice, too."

"Are you dating anyone?"

"No. You?"

"No. So, since it's snowing, and the roads are icy, and since I have the day off, will you wait until tomorrow to leave?"

It was almost like he was asking her out on a date. But she'd been burned before. Did he want more from her than she was willing to give? "Zack, what's going on?"

"What do you mean?"

She didn't appreciate it that he was playing dumb. "Come on, please tell me the truth. Why are you going out of your way for me? Why are you being so nice?"

A flicker of doubt—and hurt?—appeared in his gaze. "I don't have an agenda, Leah. I promise you that. Fact is, I just want to see you some more."

Relief made her knees weak, but valiantly, she hardened her heart. If she'd ever learned anything in her twenty years, it was to be careful. Especially with her heart.

Carefully putting on the brakes before things sped up

between them, she said, "You know, we don't know each other at all."

"I'm a police officer."

The way he puffed up his chest when he said that, so full of righteous indignation, made her smile. "And I work at a coffeehouse. But knowing someone's job doesn't mean we know them. Right?"

"Point taken." He sighed; ran a hand through his dark blond hair, messing it up just enough for Leah to see that there were darker streaks hiding underneath.

"Leah, I should have just answered you right away instead of getting my feelings hurt. You are exactly right to not trust me. So, here we go. No, I don't do this often. Actually, I've never asked a stranded girl out before."

The way he characterized her made Leah smile. "Ever?"

"Ever. I like my job, Leah. I like helping people. And being a patrol officer is demanding." He paused again—seemed to struggle to find the right words. "Until I met you, I never once considered dating someone I've met while working. But then, again, I'd never met you before."

His honest words melted her heart more than any polished flirtatious line ever could have. She began to feel trusting of him.

And even more surprising . . . well, she, too, didn't want to say goodbye to him. Not yet.

Even though she knew Melody was alone at the inn.

"You know, the roads do look bad," she said slowly. "And, I'm still a little shaken from the accident."

"That's a common consequence."

"So, Officer Littleton, if it's okay with you, I think I

better stay here another day. You know, just to be on the safe side."

"That's a smart decision, miss," he said before his solemn demeanor melted into pure pleasure. "I can't tell you how happy I am to hear you say that."

"So what would you like to do?"

"Today, I thought maybe we could just go to a movie or something. The storm is supposed to get worse before it gets better. But tomorrow morning, I'd like to take you by my parents' place. It's on the way to I-71. They have beagle puppies. Any chance you want to see a litter of six five-week-old pups?"

All feelings of unease dissipated in an instant. This was why he was so special. He wanted to show her puppies?

But just to be sure things were on the safe side, Leah took care to look at him sideways. "Will your parents be there?"

He held up a hand. "Of course."

"Then, yes, Zack, I'd love to go to the movies today and see those puppies tomorrow before I take off."

"You drive a hard bargain, Leah Dillon."

"Is that a bad thing?"

"Not at all," he said with a grin. Which, of course, made her smile, too.

December 22, 11:00 A.M.

As the icy pellets turned into fluffy flakes, Katie turned her attention to the girls and one of their favorite snowy-day treats: pretzels.

"How come we only make pretzels when it's cold outside, Katie?" Mary asked.

"I'm not sure. Maybe because it's what your *grossmammi* did with me. It's a snowy day tradition," she mused as she carefully measured three quarters of a cup of warm water, then added it to the bowl filled with yeast, sugar, and salt. As Mary and Hannah stood by, she next measured out bread flour, then handed a wooden spoon to her oldest stepdaughter. "Stir, dear."

Mary did, easily, and Hannah was already preparing for her favorite part—kneading. Her little fingers flexed, eager to grab at the dough. Little by little, they crept forward, ready to snatch it from the bowl and begin to make it elastic. "Now, Mamma?"

"Not quite. Patience, Hannah," she murmured, feeling her whole being smile with contentment. She'd been married to Jonathan over a year; and while Mary would most likely never call her anything but "Katie," already Hannah had adopted her as her own—and she was "Mamma," too.

Just as Katie felt in her heart "Mother" to Hannah and Mary, Jonathan's sweet daughters.

"Are we ready now?" Mary asked.

Katie peeked into the bowl. The dough was mixed together as well as could be done with a wooden spoon. After lightly flouring the countertop, she nodded. "Ready."

Eagerly Mary plopped the dough on the counter, and neatly divided it in half. Then she and Hannah got to work kneading the dough.

Katie stood to the side, watching in amusement as Hannah lasted all of four minutes before her arms and hands grew tired. Without a word, she stepped to Hannah's side and continued the chore.

When the dough looked almost shiny, Katie neatly divided it into six sections, then helped the girls form the clumps into long ropes.

Anna came in just as Katie was helping Hannah form her second pretzel. "Oh, yum. What a perfect day for pretzels."

Katie chuckled. "Mary and I were just discussing how snow seems to make baking much more tempting."

With a fierce look of concentration, Mary set her third pretzel on the greased baking sheet. "All of mine are done, Katie."

"Crack the egg, then. We'll need to make an egg wash, *jah?*"

"An egg wash?" Hannah giggled.

"It's what it is called."

"Like they're taking a bath!"

Katie played along. "Even pretzels need to bathe, *jah?*"

Mary grinned and carefully dipped the pastry brush into the egg-and-water mixture, then brushed the first pretzel. Beside her, Hannah looked like she couldn't seem to do more than giggle.

Anna looked fondly at Hannah. "Though I had been worried about what the holidays would be like with all the family and guests, I have to say I'm enjoying the company so much."

"I, as well. It's times like this that I think the Lord is reminding me to concentrate on the moment instead of the plans that fall through."

"So, things are better?"

"Perhaps." Katie shrugged. "It was wrong of me to want to hold on to our traditions so tightly. I should have known sharing our family activities wouldn't make them less special. Actually, they seem to make them seem more special, seen through another's eyes."

"I can vouch for that," Anna said, a dreamy look in her eyes. "When I first stayed here, I found a lot of comfort in your home. Even dusting furniture seemed different because I felt like I was important. Like I belonged. Everyone likes to feel that way, I think."

"You are right." Looking toward the door, a lump grew in Katie's throat. "I need to apologize to our guests."

"Maybe not."

"No, I think I do. Christmas is a time of sharing, and joy and Grace. There's no better time to entertain family and friends than now. It was wrong of me to forget."

As the girls continued to giggle and *bathe* pretzels, Anna nodded to the door. "Why don't you go do that now, then?"

"Now?"

"I have things under control here, and Eli is sleeping. Go apologize, then come back and we'll work on a project or two."

"All right, I will." She turned away and strode to the dining room before she could change her mind.

Chapter 11

December 22, 3:00 P.M.

"Excuse me," Katie said as she entered the dining room. "Melody, may I speak with you for a moment?"

Levi watched Melody turn to Katie in surprise. "Of course." When she stayed seated, Levi felt his admiration for her continue to grow. At first glance, Melody had seemed a fragile thing. But now he was learning she was far stronger than he'd realized. Whatever had brought her here had to have been difficult, but she wasn't dwelling on her problems.

In fact, she seemed more eager to push her problems away than to dwell on disappointments. Her fortitude drew him to her in a way he never imagined.

Katie paused next to the table. "So, may we go into another room, where we can talk privately?"

After glancing Levi's way, Melody shook her head. "Actually, if you don't mind, I'd just as soon as talk here. I'm comfortable." She patted her belly. "And comfortable with Levi here, too."

When she looked at him for reassurance, he nodded. "We've become *gut* friends."

Katie swallowed. "Oh. Well, then, all right." She darted a glance his way as she sat.

"I know I've given you every cause to believe that is how I think, but it isn't true. Usually I never think of this place as my own."

Melody frowned. "I'm confused."

Levi was as well, but he held his tongue. He was interested in what Katie Lundy had to say . . . and how Melody would react to it.

"Fact is, this isn't my home, not really."

"But you grew up here . . ."

"I grew up in an inn. We are used to having visitors. In fact, we've welcomed the company. A little more than a year ago, I married and moved away. Now I have a new home."

Melody raised her eyebrows. Levi felt just as confused. When she continued to seem tongue-tied, he spoke. "Is that what you wanted to tell her?"

"No. I wanted to apologize. For my behavior," she sputtered, her voice shaky. "When you first arrived, I was unforgivably rude. I want you to know that I am truly sorry for it."

Katie's apology embarrassed Levi. Surely it would have been better to have just not said anything at all?

"Please don't worry," Melody responded.

"I will. Melody, this won't make up for my attitude, but I will share that over the last year, our family has had a lot of changes. I married, so did Anna. So did Jonathan's sister Winnie. We've gone from being three single girls to three married women. And all during the fall, we've looked forward to these two weeks to be together again."

"Without guests."

"*Jah.*"

Though Levi appreciated the apology, he didn't necessarily feel Katie was making things better. He also didn't like how ill at ease Melody looked.

Surely she had enough on her plate without the burden of being Katie's uninvited guest. "If it was so important to you, you should have made note of that on your reservation schedule," he said more gruffly than he'd intended.

"You're right. However, we never hosted guests over Christmas before. Not ever. So, I guess Anna and Henry didn't think to do that. Anyway, I've come to realize that I've been unfair and I'm sorry."

"I'm sorry I'm ruining your week," Melody said.

New pain and chagrin entered her expression. "Please don't say that. Please don't even think that. In the short time you've been here, you both have become more like friends than mere guests. Now, why . . . I couldn't imagine you leaving."

Levi didn't doubt Katie's sincerity. There was something in her eyes that spoke of an inner turmoil that had been put to rest.

Melody must have felt the same way, because she smiled. "I'm thankful for that. I don't know where else I'd go."

"I don't know what has happened between you and your man, but, for now, please just relax and be glad here."

Levi blinked as Melody turned white. "My man?"

Katie's blue eyes flashed with pain. "Oh, for heaven's sakes. There I go again, saying things I shouldn't. I've really messed this up, haven't I? Just ignore me."

For a moment, Melody felt frozen as Katie's words slammed into her. "Are you speaking of my baby's father?" she said slowly, though the question was an unnecessary one. There was no doubt what—and who—Katie was speaking about.

"Well, yes. But like I said, it's none of my business . . ."

"I don't have a man," Melody said quickly. Now she was well aware of Levi's curious look her way as well. "The man who . . . um, well. See, I . . . I won't ever have anything to do with him. Because he is in jail."

Next to her she sensed Levi flinch.

Katie was far more verbal. "In jail? My word, what did he do?"

Well, perhaps it was time to tell the truth. The whole truth.

Suddenly, it was so easy to tell her secret. Perhaps because she was slowly starting to realize that it was part of her past? Part of who she was now? Never would she be able to put it in a place to pretend that it didn't matter.

Because it would always matter.

"The man . . . he raped me," she said softly, feeling

proud of herself for hardly stumbling over the statement. "He raped me, and then he raped another woman a few days later. She was brave enough to press charges. That is why he is in jail."

As stunned silence met her story, Melody felt relief instead of embarrassment. She'd thought that keeping her secret deep within herself would free her, but the opposite had been true. It had only weighed her down.

Perhaps Katie Lundy had been right. Perhaps all of them in this house had become more than guests and innkeepers. Perhaps they'd become friends.

Slowly, Levi reached for her hand. Tears were in his eyes. Melody waited for him to look at her differently . . . most people had in her town. But what she saw in his blue eyes was the sweetest acceptance. "Never had I imagined such a thing," he murmured.

Willing herself not to cry, she shrugged. "Why would you?"

Katie wasn't even attempting to hold back tears. "Melody, I'm so sorry."

"I know. I am, too." She squeezed Levi's hand; half waited for him to pull his away. But he did not. Instead, his large palm warmed her own. Comforted her.

As the silence lengthened, she tried to smile, to make the tension in the room ease at least a little bit. Because the alternative would be to keep it there with them all. Painful and loud. Looking at her hand encased in Jonathan's she said, "To be honest, I hadn't planned to tell any of you. I don't like to speak of it."

"Of course not," Levi said quickly.

She raised her head, feeling stronger than she was used to. "But I guess I didn't want you thinking the worst of me."

Still holding her hand, Levi murmured, "I never . . ."

Katie shook her head slowly. "You humble me. First, I didn't think the worst. I don't even know what the 'worst' is. All of us have things in our past that we'd like to forget. Some are our fault, some are at the hands of others. But beside all that, I am honored you thought enough of me to speak of it. I don't think I've ever met a braver person."

"I wouldn't call myself brave." All she'd done was survive—that was surely nothing to be proud of.

"I disagree," Katie said. "I don't know what else to say except that I promise I will now try doubly hard to make up for my earlier behavior. Will you please let me try?"

"Of course."

Slowly, Katie stood up. "Thank you. I'm grateful. Now, may I get you two more tea or coffee?"

Melody glanced Levi's way. What would she see? Remorse? Embarrassment? "Do you care to sit here any longer, Levi?"

But instead of seeing any negative thing, she only saw care in his expression. "I would enjoy more hot coffee."

"And I'd enjoy tea."

When she and Levi were alone again, Melody felt the silence like a vise to her chest. Perhaps telling him had been the wrong thing, after all?

She attempted to make a joke. "Well, now, I think my ears are burning. I would guess Katie is telling my news to everyone in the kitchen right now."

"Perhaps. Does them knowing bother you?"

"Usually it does. All I get at home is whispers and comments. Or looks of condemnation and pity. I had hoped for a break from that. It's one of the reasons I came here for Christmas."

"I know what that is like."

"You do?"

"It's nothing I care to speak of, if you don't mind. I'd far rather talk about you. Melody, do you mind if I ask you a question?"

"No."

"Are you okay?"

She knew what he was asking. Was she all right after sharing her story. Was she all right after everything? "Sometimes I am." Then, feeling that she sounded too sorry for herself, she amended her words. "And physically, I am fine. The doctor has said I've been blessed with an easy pregnancy."

"Blessed," he mumbled. Like he couldn't imagine a child born out of such circumstances could be seen as anything but a scar.

"We have to see the daylight where we can, *jah*?" she said softly. "Every day can't be cloudy and gloomy."

A muscle in his jaw worked. "And the baby . . ."

"The nurses say it is okay, too."

"I imagine it was quite a surprise."

"You imagine right. I didn't realize for a long time what was happening to me. I had no idea what to expect."

"What are you going to do with the baby when it's born? Will you give it up for adoption?"

She curved her hands around her stomach. "Oh, no. I'm

going to keep him or her," she said firmly. Realizing at that very moment nothing could be more true. "This baby is a part of me."

"But it's also of the . . . man." Looking at her worriedly, he whispered. "You don't fear it will be a reminder?"

Melody flinched but kept her head high. "Yes. But I think it will also be a reminder to me that the Lord doesn't do anything without a reason. Perhaps one day I'll discover what His reasons were for me to have this child."

Levi nodded. "Yes, one day we'll all look forward to discovering the Lord's reasons, I suppose."

Katie bustled in minutes later, her mother right behind her. Each carried a teapot and a fresh mug.

"Melody, hot tea has always made me feel better on the most dreary of days," Mrs. Brenneman said gently. "And Mr. Bender, the coffee is fresh. I hope you will find it to your liking."

Next to her, Katie looked ready to speak when Anna came through the doors, too. "I have hot pretzels," she said with a smile. "Fresh from the oven. I hope you both will enjoy them."

"We shall," Levi promised. "I'm sure we shall enjoy them very much."

When the ladies left again, and only the two of them sat together, silence stretched between them. Taut, unsure.

Neither seemed to have anything to say.

Melody wondered if, perhaps, she had already said too much.

Chapter 12

December 23, 4:00 A.M.

Oh, but sometimes she felt as if she could see her stomach grow bigger by the minute. Melody groaned as she dried her hands and turned off the bathroom light. As she waddled down the hall—as she was now doing every two hours—she felt as big as a mountain.

And twice as old. No longer did her body seem like her own; instead, it seemed to be owned by a wee baby in her belly, and she was at its beck and call. Tonight, the baby seemed to have a fierce need to go push on her bladder.

As she returned to her room, her blurry, sleepy eyesight righted itself. Out of habit, she glanced at the clock. Four A.M.

It was too early by most *Englischers'* standards, but for

the Amish, not so much. Melody knew before long she'd hear footsteps of Mr. Brenneman or Henry as the men lumbered down the stairs to attend to the farm animals.

Soon, Mrs. Brenneman would wake and she'd prepare breakfast. Such was their way.

It had been the same at Melody's home, too. Her family of four rose before dawn and worked to get their chores completed as competently as possible.

May was their gardener and canner. In the spring, she rose early with her beloved plants and seedlings and coaxed them to yield more fruits and vegetables. Summer and fall brought hours of harvesting the bounty. Her father, who had found a lot of work making beautiful custom kitchen cabinets in rich peoples' homes, would tend to the horse and buggy; then, after a quick breakfast, would ride his bike to his workshop.

And their mother, the heart of their home, polished and swept. She made everyone's meals and organized their lives. She sewed and helped watch a neighbor's children three days a week.

Melody was the baker. By all accounts, she baked bread better than the other women in the house. So each morning, she'd rise and prepare another batch of either Friendship bread or yeast bread. And then she, too, would leave for work.

Until recently, she had left on foot.

As the memory tried to resurface, Melody pushed it away. She'd already talked about it with Levi and Katie. Surely her mind didn't need to revisit things again?

With a sigh, she moved to the rocking chair. Rocked back and forth, tried to clear her mind. Tried to only think of good things, like the way her family used to laugh at supper.

How good it used to be.

Before she'd been attacked, their home had been an organized one. A close one. A happy, if not terribly fun-filled, and at least content, way of life. And then, one Friday evening, everything had changed.

May later told her that an elderly couple heard her cries for help and rushed to her side. Melody vaguely remembered the lady's kind face assuring her that the worst was over. Soon, a police woman arrived on the scene and summoned an ambulance. Later, another officer had gone to her parents and told them the news.

Her parents and May had ridden in the back of a police car to the hospital. They'd been questioned by detectives and given updates by nurses. All three had stayed by her side for the night she'd stayed there. Never did they utter a word of complaint. But somehow their family had changed.

And became more strained when Melody learned she was carrying a baby.

Sometimes, her mother said that the hardest part to deal with was the knowledge that a lifetime of innocence could be ruined in mere minutes. That a lifetime of prayer and good works could be overlooked in a flash.

Every so often, Melody liked to think of her family as a beautiful puzzle that had been put together carefully, each piece fitting just right. Her rape had destroyed the picture, thrown her family into disarray, strewn into a thousand pieces.

Of course, the only thing to do had been to try to pick each part up, one at a time . . . only to find that some pieces were gone. Lost. And that picture would never be the same.

In her room, rocking, Melody wondered if she could ever forgive herself for that.

December 23, 10:00 A.M.

Leah liked Zack's family from the moment she saw them shoveling their driveway together. They had on matching blue-and-white ski jackets and looked as athletic and fit as their son.

"Why isn't Jack out here doing this?" Zack said as soon as he parked his truck off to the side.

"Your brother had to go to work," his dad explained. "But don't worry, we've got it."

"I'll finish it up," Zack said, already pulling on his gloves. "This is Leah, the gal I called y'all about. Why don't you take her on in?"

"Glad to meet you, Leah," his mom said. "I'm Pam. This is Tom."

Tom waved a snow-covered glove while Zack looked her way. "Will you be okay for a few minutes?"

Leah couldn't help it, she was charmed. It was so cute to see how well Zack got along with his parents. "I'll be fine."

"The rest of this won't take too long," Tom called out as Leah started walking toward the house after Pam. "I'll have Zack back to you in a jiffy."

Leah grinned as Zack volleyed a snowball at his father. "Honestly, Dad—"

Pam shook her head. "Don't mind my husband. He likes to tease our oldest. Zack is always so serious."

"It's fun to see," Leah said. For years, it had been just she and her mom. She'd almost forgotten what it had been like when her parents were still married. "And thank you for letting me come out here."

As they walked into the shelter of the garage, Pam smiled kindly. "We're happy to meet you, though sad about the circumstances. I'm sorry you're stuck here in Louisville."

"It would have been worse if I hadn't met your son."

"He does have a nice way about him," his mother agreed. "All right. Let me get my boots off and then we'll get inside where it's warm."

Leah unlaced her boots and then followed Pam into a sunny blue-and-white kitchen. Flower-painted tiles dotted the walls and blue gingham curtains framed the windows. Instantly, Leah felt at home.

"How about hot chocolate?"

"That would be great, thank you."

As Zack's mother bustled around, heating up water and pouring mix into mugs, she directed Leah to the pantry for marshmallows.

Pam had just finished telling Leah about her job as a school secretary and Tom's job for the fire department when the two men joined them.

"We're kind of big into public service," Zack said when she handed him his own hot chocolate. "Jack is an EMT, like I used to be."

"I guess this is the best place to be if I ever have a problem, then," she teased. "Someone here could always fix it."

"Yeah. I think that's kind of our way. All of us hate sitting around, waiting on other people," Tom explained. "We'd kind of rather take care of things ourselves."

"Or maybe, we're gluttons for punishment," Pam quipped.

After finishing their drinks, Zack stood up. "So, are you ready to see some puppies?"

"Of course."

"Be careful, Leah," his mom warned. "They're so cute, you're going to want one."

As she followed Zack down the hall, she looked at him with a new perspective. Little by little, the man beside her kept revealing a new side to her, and she had to admit she was intrigued. Not only had he helped her, but it looked like helping others was a basic part of his life.

"I like your parents."

"Thanks. I like them, too."

"I liked learning more about you from your mom. You've done some pretty incredible things as a highway patrol officer."

He looked down. "I was just doing my job, Leah."

"You seem embarrassed. Are you?"

"I just don't think my job is anything special. Not like yours. You're going to have the ability to influence a lot of people as a guidance counselor."

"Maybe I will. That is, if I can get a job." Now she was

the one feeling uncomfortable. While it was true that she had big plans, he had already accomplished so much, and only a few years older.

Something flickered in his eyes. A new expression that told so much. That he understood, and was glad that she, too, wasn't the type to brag about achievements.

The hall ended in a small sunroom. Instead of a door opening into the area, a baby gate blocked the passage. "Here's where Trixie and her pups are." Eyeing the gate a little warily, he said, "This is a little high. My mom bought it at a garage sale, so it can't be unlatched. Do you think you can step over it?"

"Without a problem," she said. "I'm short but capable."

"Somehow that sounds about right," he said with a smile. But still, he reached out for her arm as she clambered over the gate.

As she grasped it, Leah thought it felt warm and solid. Like it was used to carrying burdens. Slowly, she met his gaze. For a moment, she wished he'd keep his hand on her arm. Or let it slip down to her hand and grasp it.

What was happening between them? They seemed to be rolling head over feet into a relationship without either of them really pushing. Their conversations were getting deeper, more meaningful, all at dizzying speed.

She was extremely grateful for the pup that toddled over and explored her ankle. "Oh, Zack!" she cried, crouching down to the tiny brown and white ball of fur.

While Zack merely looked on, it was the puppy that demanded an answer. "Yip!"

Reaching out, she gently patted its back, afraid to scare

it. But it was no scaredy-cat. "Yip!" it cried again; then, with a spin, darted back to its brothers and sisters.

Leah was completely, utterly in love.

"Zack, they're so cute! I don't know how you'll ever let them go."

He grinned as he knelt down next to the box. "It's hard. There's nothing cuter than a puppy."

Leah figured she would have a hard time topping that statement. The pups were extremely cute, and their mother, a pretty tricolored beagle, looked as proud as any human mom. Her chocolaty brown eyes automatically went to Zack and her tail thumped twice.

His hand looked gentle as he rubbed Trixie's head. "How you doing, girl? Those kids driving you crazy yet?"

As Trixie thumped her tail again, Leah scooted a little closer to Zack. Soon, the adventurous pup who'd greeted her went back toward its mom. With a tiny push, it nudged its way in for some milk.

Leah tried to count the pups, but it took some doing. They were in a puppy clump. Some were nursing, others were asleep. Each one was cuter than the next. After a few minutes, a few left Trixie's side and greeted Zack.

Knowing how protective mother dogs were, Leah stayed still, letting Zack be the guide. And that was okay, too, because seeing Zack Littleton in this way was mesmerizing. His hazel eyes gleamed as he let one of the pups chew on his finger. He laughed as another yipped and plopped on its rear.

"They're wonderful, Zack," she said. Not daring to add that she thought he was pretty wonderful, too.

Zack looked at Leah and smiled. "I thought you'd like them. Makes you almost forget it's snowing outside."

"Almost."

When Trixie thumped her tail again, Leah reached out her hand to pet her, then stilled. She didn't want to worry the new mother.

"It's okay," Zack murmured. "Trixie trusts me. Just go ahead and say hi to her first."

Following Zack's lead, she petted the beagle. "Your babies are beautiful," she whispered, then grinned Zack's way as one little puppy stretched and walked over to inspect her. Before she knew it, two others yipped and whined, and then jumped and raced her way.

Zack laughed. "Oh, you're in for it now. They want to play."

Pushing her legs out in front of her, Leah picked up the puppy who'd just yipped. The little pup was pudgy and squirmy. Unable to help herself, she cuddled him close. "Oh, he smells like a puppy."

Zack reached over and rubbed the puppy's head. "I knew you'd love them." He paused. "Listen, I'm going to do a little bit of cleaning up and check my email before we get going. Will you be okay for a few minutes?"

"Playing with puppies? Take your time."

Soon, all six wanted attention, and Leah literally had her hands full of wiggling, squirming pups. She picked up one after the other as Zack cleaned up shredded, soiled newspaper and refilled the water bowl. Soon, even Trixie got to her feet and stretched.

"She wants to go out. I'll be right back."

"Take your time." Leah shooed him away. "I'll be fine. Take all the time you want."

As he left the room, she realized with some surprise that she was starting to feel more at ease with him. Maybe it was because she'd met his family. Maybe it was because he was a police officer. Or maybe, it was just because he was Zack.

 *Chapter 13*

December 23, 11:00 A.M.

"We couldn't stay away another day," Winnie Miller said when she arrived at the inn with Sam and a suitcase full of clothes.

Looking at his wife fondly, Sam chuckled. "Just so you know, Winnie means that literally. If I hadn't started loading up the buggy right after breakfast, I'm afraid she would have started walking over here."

"I wasn't that bad. Well, maybe I was," Winnie said with a grin as she followed Katie and Anna into the entryway of the home. "I've just been on eggshells wondering what you all have been doing this morning without me." She looked around. "What project are you working on today? Quilts, maybe? Cookies?"

"I believe the plan is to make doughnuts and wrap up Christmas presents for the girls," Anna said. "And we're going to have some venison stew. The men have been busy hunting."

Katie smiled at her sister-in-law's quick pace as she followed them into the hearth room to greet Mary and Hannah.

After admiring the napkins the girls were finishing up for their grandmother, Winnie eyed Katie more closely. "Are you all right? How's Eli?"

"A little fussy today, if you want to know the truth. Jonathan's rocking him in our room. I'm hoping he's just out of sorts because of all the people."

Winnie winked. "That's understandable. I've been known to be out of sorts from time to time as well."

Thinking of when Winnie had been recuperating from the fire and had been confined to a wheelchair, Katie said, "Perhaps my Eli takes after his aunt? He doesn't like to be confined one bit."

"Let's hope he never has to have his leg in a cast, then," Winnie teased. She looked to continue when Melody stuck her head in.

When she spied the three of them, Melody quickly stepped out. "I'm sorry. I was just looking for my book."

Still mindful of Melody's news, and her past behavior, Katie rushed to invite her. "Would you like to join us? We're going to make lard cakes soon."

"Thank you, but no. I seem to be all thumbs today. Who knows what trouble I'd get into near hot oil. I'm going to sit and read for a bit before I go outside."

That surprised Katie. "Outside? It's barely above freezing."

"I know, but the sun is out. And, well . . . Levi offered to walk with me this afternoon."

"Ah. Well, I imagine a little bit of fresh air will do you good."

As Anna walked off with Melody to help her find her book, Winnie turned to Katie. "How are things going? Does she seem to be settling in better?"

"I think so." Briefly she told Winnie about hearing Melody cry at night . . . and then also how she noticed Melody and Levi eating cookies together the night before. "Perhaps she had been right to come here for the holiday. She certainly needed to rest."

Winnie, being Winnie, jumped from the story to her quick conclusion.

"Or, perhaps, there was more guiding here than simply a need to rest. Perhaps God put them both here for a reason."

Katie did believe in the Lord guiding them . . . but she also believed in chance, too. "We've lots of people who stay here at the same time. Usually, it's of no consequence."

"But it could be. You never know," she added, her voice turning dreamy. "Why, I think God put me in the hospital right next to Samuel's place of work for a reason . . ."

"Perhaps," Katie allowed. "Or, perhaps not. You're such a romantic, Win."

"Only recently. But truly, being romantic is a good thing, ain't so?"

"Oh, Win. You do make me laugh. Come help me roll out dough for the lard cakes."

* * *

December 23, 11:00 A.M.

The most wondrous things were happening at the Brenneman Bed and Breakfast. Sometime between when she'd first arrived in such an exhaustive state—and now, just two days later—Melody had begun to feel at peace.

Perhaps it was the homespun comfort of the inn, with the fresh scent of greenery draping the front door and the trio of candles decorating the front reception desk.

Perhaps it was the friendship she observed among the Brenneman family. They had a bustling, comfortable way about them. Mr. and Mrs. Brenneman were the obvious heads of the house, but they easily worked side by side with Henry and Katie. Yes, there was real love there.

Or, perhaps, what affected Melody most was the romantic love between the newlyweds. Seeing Katie's blue eyes shine whenever she saw her husband made Melody smile, too.

And watching Henry's ever-so-patient demeanor with his Anna truly made Melody sigh with longing. It was so obvious that these matches were made in heaven, and that they were fulfilling partnerships in every way possible.

And while seeing that should have made Melody feel even more nostalgic for the things that could never be, right here, right now at the inn . . . why, everything suddenly felt possible. Suddenly all her despair was leaving her.

But perhaps much of that optimism had to do with the man beside her. Levi Bender was secretive and quiet. His eyes seemed to see far more than he let on. And it was obvious that his feelings ran deep. But it was because of that pain—not in spite of it—that a sense of tranquility had been created between them.

Melody was grateful for it as they bundled up and walked outside.

There weren't too many places to go, not really. It was either walk around the property or go into the woods. Or do what they were doing now, which was walk up and down the long, meandering driveway. Levi was one of the few men she'd ever met who didn't seem to mind her small stature, or her slow walking pace. In fact, it felt as if he could have let their little walk take all day, if that's what she needed. Every so often when she would stop, he would hold out a hand just in case she needed his support.

As he was doing at the moment. "Do you mind the snow?" he asked when she stopped to stomp one of her boots. "Is it too icy for you? Do you want to go back?"

His conciliatory manner was so sweet, she shook her head. "I don't mind the snow at all, and it doesn't feel too icy to me. Actually, it does my body good to get out and about."

"I feel the same way."

Melody hid a smile. She'd been talking about her very large condition. She was so big and uncomfortable now, sitting or lying down brought precious little relief. "Are you used to sitting around less?"

"Very much so. At the factory, I'm constantly in motion. I mean, I'm busy there."

"You work in a garage-door factory, don't you?"

"*Jah.*"

"Do you like it?"

"I do, well enough." He shrugged. "It's a *gut* job. I not only help build the doors, I sometimes am asked to assist in managing the men."

"They must respect you."

"Perhaps." Lines around his eyes deepened as he smiled. "Like I said, I like working there. I've worked there almost ten years now. The men there are good and easy to work with. And fair, too. There's no one who makes things difficult or who doesn't want to do his part. That's a rarity, I think."

"Are they all Amish?"

"*Nee*. We're about half and half, which makes life interesting. We joke around with each other. And laugh a lot, too. All of that makes the days go by fast."

They continued to walk down the gravel driveway. There wasn't much to see, beyond snowbanks and bare thickets of woods. Around them, the tall oaks and maples were void of branches. Every so often, a vehicle's engine could be heard. But other than that, they were completely alone.

That's when Melody realized two things. One, he was the first man she'd been alone with in almost nine months, and she wasn't afraid. Secondly, she was enjoying this man's company. Enjoying his self-deprecating humor.

Stopping again, she looked at him in wonder. "Levi, it is *wunnerlich*, but now I think I can actually imagine you laughing."

"And how is that strange?"

"When we first met—all of two days ago—I don't know if I could. You seemed very sullen."

The twinkling in his eyes vanished, making her wish that she'd held her tongue. "I had a lot on my mind," he finally said when they started walking again.

They had reached the end of the driveway. In unison, they turned and started back. Now the beautiful oak sign announcing the entrance to the Brenneman Bed and Breakfast greeted them like a symbol of hope. Drawing them closer.

Perhaps the right thing to do would be to drop the subject. To not push Levi. But Melody found she couldn't. Now she had no secrets left. The man beside her knew she was with child, and that this child was a product of the most terrible of things.

But he also knew that she'd survived, was stronger for it. So she pushed. "Is your mind burdened because it's Christmas?"

"Partly."

"But not all . . ."

She misstepped and almost tripped on a rock. He held out his hand and supported her elbow. And finally answered. "Christmas is part of my problem. But no, not all."

"Do you want to share?"

"Not especially."

"You might feel better for it."

"My, you're being direct now."

She couldn't deny that. "You don't have to answer, of course. If you choose not to, I'll understand." She paused, trying to put into words what was jumbled in her brain.

"But I think something tragic happened to you. And I know what dealing with that feels like."

"Yes, I guess you do . . ."

She smiled, frankly surprised at herself for her whole attitude. "Now that I've told you my worst, I suppose it is easy to be open."

"I am sorry for you."

"I know."

"And . . . I am grateful that you aren't afraid of me." Under the brim of his black hat, Levi's hazel eyes darkened, revealing a mix of emotions. Tenderness and caution warred in their depths, drawing her closer.

As did his voice. "I . . . I would never hurt you, Melody."

"I know that, too," she murmured softly. "Believe me, if I thought you would, I would have left the inn right away."

Again, her frankness seemed to take him off guard. "I hope I never make you feel worry or pain."

Like his gaze, there was something in his voice that drew her to him. For a moment, she yearned to reach out to him. Almost wished he'd wrap a comforting arm around her shoulder.

Stunned by the direction her mind was taking her, she attempted to lighten things up. "I'll only feel pain if we walk for another hour. Our stroll is showing me that even the shortest walks can be tiring. I'm a little winded."

"We can go slower . . ."

"Oh, no. I'm fine. Just big and pregnant." They were nearing the inn. In twenty or so more steps, they would reach the front door. And then their private time together would end. "So . . . why did you leave your home for Christmas, Levi?"

"I wanted a respite from my life."

"I can understand that. I did, too. But there was another reason, wasn't there?"

"There was."

She took a chance. "Levi, what were you running away from?"

He swallowed hard. "My memories."

"Bad ones?"

"Bad and good."

They were almost at the house. Through the windows, Melody could see Mrs. Brenneman and Katie's two daughters sewing. Through another, Mr. Brenneman was visible, whittling.

In mere moments, they would no longer be alone. This closeness would dissipate. They'd meld into the rest of the group . . . go separate ways. The opportunity to talk openly would be gone.

"Levi, what is your bad memory?"

He hung his head. "I'm reluctant to tell you."

Was he guarding himself? Or more worried about how she would receive the news?

Fearing that, she touched his arm with one mittened hand. "I promise, there's nothing you could say that would shock me."

As if in slow motion, he turned her way. "On Christmas Eve, two years ago, my wife Rosanna and our baby died," he said bleakly. "She'd wanted to have our baby in the hospital, but I saw no need for that. My mother and sisters had delivered at home . . ." His voice drifted off, as if the rest of his thoughts were too painful to share.

But then, before she could say a word . . . before she could actually reach out like she yearned to . . . Before she could press a hand to his arm and assure him that he didn't need to say another word . . . Before she could apologize for prying, he spoke.

"There was a problem. So much blood." He swallowed. "The midwife couldn't help—Rosanna . . . my Rosanna needed a blood transfusion. But of course, we couldn't do that." Looking as bleak as the empty plains beyond the house, he continued. "And so, she died. They both did."

They were at the front steps now. Though she still stood, frozen, Levi climbed the three steps. When he reached the door, he looked her way. His eyes now looked vacant. Curiously empty.

"And so that is what I am running away from, Melody. My ghosts. Christmas. And the knowledge that my arrogance—my heavy-handed pride—killed my wife and child."

He turned the handle and stepped inside.

Leaving Melody to realize she'd been a liar. Here, she'd thought no one's words, no one else's story, could ever shock her.

But she'd been wrong. She was stunned to the core.

Turning on her heel, she started walking again.

Chapter 14

December 23, noon

Levi strode by the whole family without a word and marched up the stairs like he was in a daze.

Beside Katie, Jonathan whistled low. "That there is a man who is hurting."

"Hurting or angry?" Katie asked as she watched him cross the second-floor landing, and then walk down the hall. Seconds later, they all heard him take the last bit of stairs to his attic room. A dull thud of his door let them all know he wasn't coming out anytime soon.

Still looking upward, Jonathan tilted his head to one side. "My guess is hurting. If he was angry, he'd probably be stomping more."

"Perhaps."

Katie's mom turned to the window. "Ah. Melody turned and went walking again. It looks like she's going to do another lap on the driveway."

"I hope she'll be all right. It's a long walk in the cold."

"It is." Her *mamm* frowned. "I know their business is private, but I can't help but wonder what got them both so upset. They hardly know each other."

Jonathan crossed his arms over his chest. "It does seem strange. From the looks of their faces, they were having quite a discussion. A serious one. I wonder what happened?"

"I guess we'll never know."

In Katie's arms, Eli fussed again. When he'd woken up, his cheeks were bright red and he pulled at his ears. Now no position seemed to make him happy. Katie was worrying that he might be sick.

After repositioning and gently patting his back, Katie watched Melody walk down their driveway again. "She sure is getting a lot of exercise. Oh, I hope she's not about to deliver."

Reaching out, Jonathan took the baby from her. "That has been on your mind, hasn't it?"

"I can't help but worry. It's a big event."

"Which you don't want to happen here."

"I promise, I feel much better toward our guests. I don't resent their presence any longer. But delivering a baby is a scary thing."

"Let's not borrow trouble," her mother said. Pressing a palm to the windowpane, she said, "But I will admit to being worried about Melody out there, walking alone. Katie, why don't you go see if someone can talk to her? Maybe Anna or Henry is free?"

"There's no need. I can go speak with her. That is, if you don't mind staying with Eli, Jonathan."

"Of course I don't. But do you know what you're going to say?"

"Not at all."

"You're just going to hope something comes to you?"

"Well, I will hope and pray." She smiled. "I know God is with us. I'll have a word with him while I walk out to meet Melody. Wish me well."

Jonathan pressed his lips to her brow. "Good luck, Katie. I hope you won't offend Melody while you walk."

"Thank you for your faith in me," she said sarcastically.

"Oh, I have faith in our Lord," he said with a smile. "I'm just not certain if He's going to have time to answer you right at this moment."

"He will. I'm certain of it."

Katie caught up with Melody just as she'd turned around and was facing the sign. "Hi."

Melody looked at her in wonder. "Is anything wrong?"

"I don't know. We saw Levi go upstairs in a lather and you continue walking . . . is everything okay?"

"It's fine. I just thought I'd get some exercise."

"I've walked this driveway a time or two. I can vouch for its benefits. You must be careful though, yes? You don't want to overdo it."

"This is nothing to my usual day at work. I'm on my feet all day then."

"You work in a coffee shop."

"I do. It's called Great Grinds. I make fancy coffees for people."

"Is it a good job?"

"The best. The owner, Mrs. Sheridan is a good lady. She's the one who gave me the gift certificate for here, you know. She thought I needed a break."

"I'm worried with all the commotion you aren't having much of one."

"It's good enough."

"Do you have any close friends there?"

"One. Leah. She's English, but we're very close. I feel like she could be my sister."

"I was that way with Anna. Well, almost. We didn't see each other all that much, but when we did, it was as if we'd only been apart for a day or two."

"So you had a lot in common, even though she wasn't Plain?"

"We did. And she was very different. She had adopted a way of life unlike the Plain lifestyle before she sought refuge here. At first, I was really worried she wouldn't be happy."

"She seems really happy."

"She is. She loves my brother, and I think she loves being surrounded by lots of family, too. Friends make good family, too, you know."

"Perhaps."

"So, is there anything we should do for Mr. Bender?"

"For Levi? I don't know."

"Is he upset with something here?"

"No. He's upset with something in his past."

"Ah."

"I wouldn't feel right about sharing too much, but I will say that Christmas reminds him of unhappy memories."

"Then we'll have to do our best to make new ones for him," Katie said simply, though she knew that was a very difficult thing to do. One cannot just wish away problems. They have to be dealt with, not hidden.

For a moment, she let herself think about her English friend Holly, who had gone to such lengths to find her after the end of Katie's *rumspringa*. At first, Katie hadn't wanted to see her because she'd felt guilty about her treatment of Holly's brother.

But Holly had taught her much about the power of love . . . and about forgiveness. The last time Katie had visited with Holly, her friend had shown off her engagement ring and had been full of smiles about Charlie, her fireman fiancé.

Katie and Jonathan already had plans to attend Holly's wedding.

Yes, the past always had a way of returning. Especially when it was least expected.

December 23, noon

Zack was frowning when he found her by the back door. "Leah, I looked at the weather report, and the snow is supposed to get worse. The roads are going to be difficult."

Leah felt her stomach drop. "I better not wait another moment, then. I better get going."

To her surprise, Zack reached out and took her hand. "Are you sure you really have to go to Adams County?"

"I am. Melody needs a friend."

"You can't be her friend when she returns? I'm sure she'll understand once you tell her what you've been going through."

"Zack, I hear what you're saying. I know the weather's horrible and the roads are in bad shape. But the thing of it is, Melody would never expect anyone to go out of their way for her. That's why I need to go. She needs to know someone still cares for her, no matter what." Leah paused, struggling to find another way to describe her petite, fragile friend. "She's a really sweet person."

"You are, too."

The way he looked at her—as though she was really special—made Leah feel like she was the luckiest girl in the world. "It's Christmas. Everyone should be with family and friends."

"But she made that choice to be away."

"I don't think she felt like she had a choice. I think she was trying to find peace, and the only way she thought she could find it was by running away. I can't let her be all alone."

He slumped, but still didn't look happy.

His body language spurred her to finally ask something

that she'd been pondering all day. "Zack, please don't take this the wrong way, because I really have been enjoying your company. But, why are you so concerned about me?"

"Please don't be afraid . . . but from the moment we met, I haven't been able to think of another thing. I like you a lot."

He'd been in her mind, too. But she'd been embarrassed. After all, who fell in love like that? "I like you, too." She took care to keep her tone upbeat and light.

But Zack didn't follow her lead. "From the moment I saw you leaning against your car, I wanted to get to know you better," he said seriously. "And everything I've learned has led me to want to get to know you even more. "I promise, I've never done this before. It's not like me to want to protect virtual strangers, but suddenly I'm worried about you."

"I promise I'm a good driver."

"It's everyone else I worry about. And it's about you traveling by yourself."

"Are you worried some other man is going to try to pick me up?"

"Honestly? Yes."

"Zack!"

"Don't act so surprised. You asked, and I'm telling you the truth."

"I think you're worrying a little too much."

"I can't help it. You're beautiful."

In a flash, her cheeks started to heat. His words embarrassed her. His attention was disconcerting. No one had ever called her beautiful. Leah looked at him closely. What was this man really like? Could guys really be this . . . nice?

It seemed all he wanted was for her to be safe and cared for.

"Leah, I've been turning this around in my head all day, trying to find a way to ask you. But there isn't a good way, so I'm just going to say it. Leah, how about I go with you to the Brenneman Bed and Breakfast?"

"What?"

"I'll drive you. I've got four-wheel drive; we'll be able to get through anything."

"But—"

"And I'll be the perfect gentleman. I won't even try to kiss you."

She was curiously disappointed. "You won't?"

He laughed. "I won't, if you don't want me to."

She wasn't sure what she wanted, so she left that one alone. "But what about your family? Your job?"

"I've got vacation hours. I was going to skip them and work so other guys—guys who have girlfriends and wives—could have the time off. But now I'm thinking I should have a turn, too."

"And your family?"

"They'll understand. I'm crazy about you, Leah. I want to do something for you, do something to make you smile."

"I don't know what to say."

"Then say you'll think about it."

"I'll think about it," she whispered. And smiled.

Her pulse raced a bit when he smiled right back.

Chapter 15

The tiny flakes, once interspersed in the wind and fluttering like the most delicate of dandelion fuzz, multiplied in number. As the waning sun faded behind the expanse of clouds, the storm blew in.

Rendering everything in its midst immobile.

Levi watched the swirling patterns from his window. The chaotic flakes, as they swirled and fell, twisted and blew, reminded him of the state of his mind. It, too, was in chaos.

He'd been wrong to lay his problems on Melody's slim shoulders. Dealing with Rosanna's death was his burden alone, and no one else's. He'd certainly had no business pushing his private demons her way.

He flinched as he recalled Melody's look of shock, the stiffening of her shoulders. She obviously had more than enough to worry about on her own. What had he been thinking?

Nothing more than his own selfish desires, he imagined. Ever since Rosanna had died, he'd kept all his feelings to himself. Oh, not the grief-stricken ones; those he shared with everyone in his community, her parents. And his.

But the all-encompassing thoughts of desperation— the ones that kept him up in the middle of the night, the ones that filled his mind when he didn't actively attempt to flood his thoughts with other things. Those were the things he kept private. As he well should.

Until today. And for a brief moment, he'd felt better. When he heard his words spoken aloud, he realized that perhaps it hadn't been necessary to take all the blame for Rosanna's passing. After all, the Lord was always with them, and there had been a reason He'd claimed them.

Levi knew that to be true.

So, for a brief moment in time, he'd felt his cloak of guilt lift, and he was able to look at the world in a clearheaded way. And the vision was brighter than he'd remembered.

And then he'd spied the worry and pain in Melody's expression.

And everything became dark again.

He didn't blame Melody's reaction. Not at all.

Now he was shuttered again, alone with his thoughts,

his grief and his worries. And feeling such pain—so fresh—that he worried about living his life any longer.

If God had taken Rosanna and their baby to heaven early, and Levi believed that to be true . . . what were God's reasons for leaving him alive? Even Levi didn't believe that God would unveil his wrath for the next thirty years. No man deserved to suffer for so long.

But if that wasn't the logic behind His will. What was?

Pressing his palm to the icy pane, Levi poured his heart out. "Why, Lord? Why am I still living, when my Rosanna died? What reason did you have to take our baby? What purpose do you have for me?"

The frost on the pane was cold enough to burn after a few moments, sending icy hot blades into his palm and down his arm. With a start, Levi dropped his hand to his side.

Turning away from the window, he sank to his knees. Spoke from the very depths of his soul. He had nothing to lose—having already lost what was most important. And now he was on the verge of losing his mind . . . at least it felt that way.

Unless he could connect again with the living. And that, he realized with some surprise—was what he yearned for so very much. Since he hadn't died, he wanted to live.

But he wanted to live fully, transparently with the Lord, and with others. He wanted to step out of the shadows and into his Maker's light.

Closing his eyes, he prayed. "Lord, I am yours. I am yours as I always have been. Please guide me. Please walk with me, tell me your wishes. Tell me your wants. Lord, did you direct me to this place?

"Why did you give me Melody and her willing ear when I was so determined to pretend nothing had happened?"

He breathed deep, forcing his lungs to expand and deflate in a normal rhythm, not like he was out of breath from running in a race. Little by little, a sense of peace blanketed him. And he knew without a doubt that the Lord had heard him.

"You guided me here to live again, didn't you? You guided me here to remind me what a family was, to remind me of the wonders of life, and of the wonders of renewal."

It was his wake-up call, to be sure.

It was God's Grace—giving all the love and security and hope that one could yearn for, even when one feels undeserving.

Because Rosanna and Ruth never would be forgotten. Of course, they wouldn't. But that didn't mean he had to live a forgotten life—live in the shadows, and in the past.

Wearily, he climbed to his feet. To his surprise, his cheeks were damp from shed tears. He brushed them off with his shirttail.

And stood a little straighter—

Just as he heard the knocking on his door.

"Levi? It is almost supper time," Mr. Brenneman's voice echoed through the wood. "Mr. Bender, *Levi* . . . are you all right?"

He crossed the room and opened the door. "*Jah*. I . . . am sorry, did you call from downstairs and I didn't hear?"

"Not at all," he replied, grinning. "Unlike some of my *kinner*, I'd rather not shout at the top of my lungs. I'd rather my feet did the work for me."

Before Levi could tell Mr. Brenneman that he'd be down to supper presently, the older man wandered in. "Are you finding your room comfortable?"

"Yes. It is a nice room, to be sure."

The innkeeper turned to the window with the shade pulled up. "I've always liked this view," he murmured, crossing the room and looking out. "It kind of makes you feel like a barn owl, yes?"

Now that his vision was clearer, Levi realized it was true . . . one could see for miles. Even with the snow falling down, he could see the dim lights of other houses in the distance and, farther away, the faint glow of automobiles as they made their way along the highway. "That's a good description, for sure."

John Brenneman turned to face him. "I'll ask you again. Levi, *are you all right?*"

The man's expression was open. And his searching gaze showed that he saw everything, too. He was not a man who could be lied to.

And Levi didn't want to lie.

"I don't know. Years ago, my wife and baby died in childbirth. On Christmas Eve. The memories of that night have been with me every day since then. I've felt guilty that I was alive. And I felt guilty for my part in their death."

"So you caused it?"

The direct question caught him off guard. Usually no

one said a word about that night. "Not directly," he said slowly. "I had wanted to have the birth at home. I had been obstinate that way."

"I see." For a moment, Mr. Brenneman stared out the window. Then, he turned to Levi again. "But how was their deaths your doing? What did you do?"

"Nothing on purpose." His answer was automatic, which came as a surprise. Steeling himself, he admitted the whole truth. "I insisted that my wife have the baby at home. There were complications."

"Ah." A new understanding filled his gaze. "And so you think you caused the complications?" he asked gently.

"No. The baby had moved. Or maybe it was the placenta? Anyway, we couldn't have known without a sonogram." Once again, his words echoed in his mind. *He couldn't have known.*

"Levi, it's been my experience to try not to guess why the Lord does things," he said quietly. "There has to be a reason he took them . . . and brought you here. Yes?"

"Yes. Tonight, I think I am at last realizing that."

"What changed?"

"I finally spoke to the Lord about it. Oh, not asking for forgiveness, I've done that almost every day. But finally telling him that I trusted him. That I believed in his will and his Grace."

"Sometimes that's a terrible hard thing to do, yes?"

"For me, that is true. But I feel better. And I am grateful for the opportunity to stay here. I am glad you've allowed your house to be my house this Christmas."

The corners of John's eyes crinkled as he smiled broadly.

"Oh, no, Mr. Bender. My *haus* is your home too, *jah*? For now and forever, it is your home. And especially now, at Christmas." He reached out and patted Levi's shoulder. "You should come down now, if you can. Otherwise we'll receive the wrath of the womenfolk."

"I'm in no mood for that. Let me splash some water on my face and I'll be right there."

John Brenneman had already started walking. "We'll save you a seat."

Chapter 16

December 23, 5:00 P.M.

Never had venison and pork roast and yams and green beans tasted so good, Melody reflected. Though, most certainly, the flavor of the food had as much to do with her dining partners as it did with the cooks' skills.

The long table was filled with the family and their two guests. Next to Melody sat Anna and her husband Henry; and across, their friend Winnie and her husband Sam. Next to them were Katie and Jonathan and their girls Hannah and Mary. At the ends were Mr. and Mrs. Brenneman. And to the right of Mr. Brenneman sat Levi Bender.

He had on a different shirt than he had worn when they'd gone walking. This one, a deep, dark blue, held neatly by black suspenders, matched his dark hair and beard.

And his dark hazel-colored eyes.

He turned and met her gaze. Melody felt herself flush for a moment. Flustered, she looked down at her plate again.

It wouldn't do for everyone to see her staring at him. It wouldn't do at all.

But now that she'd taken a good, long look his way, Melody couldn't help think about him.

Most certainly, Levi Bender had kidnapped her thoughts.

Yes, he was truly a handsome man. He was blessed with good skin and a muscular build that moved gracefully when he did anything.

But what really drew her eye was his quiet reserve. Now.

Before, he'd looked so angry. Angry with himself, and with her. Why, he'd hardly been able to look at her without burning her with his vehemence.

Now, of course, she understood why.

But something had changed. A true sense of peace now seemed to fill him. Every action and word appeared less wary and more open.

And then, wonder of wonders, he laughed. The sound was loud and free. Full of happiness. Not stifled at all. It encouraged her to want to laugh, too.

Actually, it encouraged a great many emotions—some long dormant. None of which involved fear. All of which included a mesmerizing longing.

Melody was so pleased by his transformation that she

almost chuckled, too. She saved face by staring at her plate. Oh, if only roasted pork actually held as much appeal!

Conversation floated around her, but she only had ears for Levi.

"Mary, your stories about school make me very glad I'm not there anymore," he said, sounding more human than ever before. "I don't know what I would have done if my classroom had housed a snake in a cage."

"I know I wouldn't have appreciated living with that creature," Mrs. Brenneman said. "I am *verra* thankful the teacher didn't ask the *kinner* to take it home on the weekends."

"I wish we could have brought it home. We liked it," Mary said.

Katie patted her stepdaughter's shoulder. "I know you did. And I know your teacher says that God loves all creatures. I'm sure he does, but I have to say that I'm still afraid of that snake."

Jonathan waved off his wife's silliness. "It was nothing. Just a simple garter snake—one that the boys in Mary's class caught and brought inside. I'm sure it rues the day it decided to venture into the schoolyard."

Levi grinned. "I'm sure your teacher rues the day she let you all keep it."

"It would have been all right if the snake didn't keep getting loose."

"I can only imagine," Katie said.

"She said we now have to keep it until spring, because it might freeze if we left it out in the snow."

"I'm afraid you are right."

The conversation floated to other topics then. The men discussed their deer hunt; Anna and Katie described the progress that had been made on a quilt. Little by little, Melody found herself participating, but only at a minimum.

She assumed the others imagined she was too shy to talk much.

But that wasn't what had stopped her. No, it was the focus of her thoughts. Levi. Now that she understood about his past. Now that she understood about his pain, she couldn't stop wishing she could get to know him better.

After dinner, she insisted on helping to clear the table. Mrs. Brenneman allowed her to carry a few plates in, but then motioned her out of the warm kitchen. "You should stay off your feet, Melody," she chided. "I heard you already went for a long walk. That's enough exercise, yes?"

Not wanting to be a bother, Melody nodded. "All right. I will go sit in the parlor."

As she walked to that room, she noticed all the men helping to clear the table and sweep. To her surprise, Sam and Henry even carried a couple of the extra chairs that they'd pulled up to the dinner table back to where they belonged.

Then Levi walked to her side. "There's a puzzle out. Would you like to work on it with me?"

She nodded. When they sat across from each other, he looked her way and smiled. "I'm actually not much for puzzles, but I wanted the chance to speak with you," he confided. "Alone."

Anticipation rose inside her. "Yes?"

He bent his head, moved two pieces this way and that. "Melody, the truth is, I wanted to tell you that I'm sorry about earlier. About what I told you during our walk."

"You're sorry you told me about your wife?"

"Yes." After pausing for a second, he finally met her gaze. "It was wrong of me to tell you so much."

"I feel just the opposite," Melody said. "I'm glad you told me what concerned you."

"But still, it was wrong to tell you such things."

"Because I'm pregnant and you don't want to worry me? Or is it because it is so painful to talk about?"

His expression gentled as he exhaled. "Both. Sometimes, Melody, I feel like you can read my mind. As a matter of fact, I was just asking myself some of those very same things. Asking and praying for guidance."

"Did you find any peace?"

He smiled then. "I like how you said that. *Peace*."

Melody only knew about searching for peace because she'd tried so hard to pray for it herself. "Peace can be a hard thing to discover," she said slowly.

"But I think prayer is helping." Now giving up all pretense of even looking at the puzzle, Levi stretched out a hand to her. When she placed her palm in his, he slowly smiled. "Prayer has helped me realize that many of my problems have lain deep within me. I believe in our Lord something fierce. I know he directs my day. I talk to him like he's my friend—because I know he is. I know He cares for me. But, Melody, I had shut him out with my pain."

She knew exactly what that felt like. "Sometimes, when the pain is so hard, it makes the world dark."

"That was how my life was. Filled with darkness instead of light. I had shut him out. As soon as I realized that if I trust him with so much, I should also trust him with my pain and burdens, too . . . and I felt better."

"I'm glad for that." Looking at their hands clasped together, thinking about how much easier it was to talk to each other, she shyly added, "Tonight, you seem different."

"I feel different, too. Can I tell you a secret?"

"Of course."

"In the back of my mind, I had been counting the hours until I would leave. I've been uncomfortable here, seeing all the other couples. This inn has been nothing that I imagined."

"For me, too. For some reason, I had hoped that I could fade into the woodwork and not be seen."

"I had thought we'd be one of many guests."

Looking at their linked fingers again, she said, "Instead, we stick out like sore thumbs."

"But now, I'm determined to enjoy each day to the fullest. I don't want to wish away Christmas. I want to enjoy these last moments of Advent and look forward to Jesus's birth with anticipation."

"I, too, am eager for that." After squeezing her hand, he released it.

"There seems to be a bond between us. Maybe it's because we both know hardship and pain. Melody, can we make a truce of some kind? Can we decide to become friends?"

"I would like that. It would be *wunderbaar, jah?*"

He grinned. "It would be *wunderbaar schee.*"

Melody smiled right back. It would be wonderful nice, indeed.

December 23, 6:30 P.M.

Leah grimaced as her mother let loose another emotional tirade. "Mother, *no*. I do not want you to meet me in Cincinnati. I'm fine."

"I don't think so. Everything you've been doing is completely out of character for you, Leah. You don't hang out with men you've hardly met. Remember what happened to Melody?"

Like she could ever forget. "This isn't the same situation, Mom. You and I both know that. Plus, I know Zack well now."

"So you say." Her voice lowered. "Are you in trouble? Do you feel like he's forcing his company on you?"

"Uh, no. Mom. I'm a sensible person. I don't do things without a reason."

"I used to think that, but now I'm not so sure. You're worrying me. I can't believe you are going to visit Melody in the company of a man you hardly know. What will she think?"

Leah prayed for patience. "Now we're worrying about Melody's opinion of me? Mom, don't you think you're taking things a little too far?"

"I don't think far enough. Please, why don't you reconsider this journey you're on?"

"I think differently. And it is a journey. I truly feel that

God has been in charge of this trip of mine since the moment I left our driveway. There's been too many coincidences to think otherwise."

"You sound like your head's in the clouds."

"Well, maybe it is." Gentling her voice, she said, "Mom . . . Zack is different. He's a good man. He's a police officer."

"That means nothing. It doesn't mean he's perfect."

"I don't want perfect."

"You should in this case. Leah, you really do need to rethink these sudden decisions of yours. I'm afraid you're going to look back on this moment and really regret it. Be smarter."

Leah knew everything her mother said made sense. She knew everything her mother said was from concern, too. Because she cared.

But that didn't mean she was right.

The strained silence that fell between them felt awkward when she hung up the phone and breathed deeply. She and her mom had rarely ever fought. Their relationship had been a unique one in Leah's circle of friends.

Usually, her mom seemed to "get" her. She usually trusted Leah, and the feeling was mutual. Leah trusted her mother's instincts about people, and about making the right choices in life. She'd always felt like she could tell her mom anything.

But this time, she regretted doing so.

Maybe it was all that coaching that her mom had done over the years, coaxing Leah to be strong and independent, persuading her to think for herself—because, right now, she felt she wasn't making a terrible mistake by going with Zack.

As Leah walked back to the truck from the gas station they had stopped at, Zack saw the look on her face. "Uh-oh. What happened?"

"Do I look that obvious? Sorry. I just got off the phone with my mother."

"And?"

"And she doesn't think it's very smart of me to go anywhere with you."

His face became a mask as he continued forward. Leah stepped to the side when he opened the passenger door for her. Then he turned to her. "Do you want to go by yourself now? If you do . . . I'd understand. We can turn around."

"I don't know," she answered quickly. Not because she wanted to do anything but go to Adams County with him. But because now, suddenly, she wondered if she had been acting too rashly.

With measured movements, he straightened and closed the truck's door, then walked around to his side. "What are you unsure about?" he asked quietly as he settled into the driver's seat.

"I guess we don't know each other all that well."

"Ah. Well, okay. Is there anything special you want to know?"

"You know that's not how it works. You don't get to know someone by asking each other twenty questions." She winced as she heard the last of her comment. She sounded sharp and shrill.

Maybe even immature.

But instead of losing patience, Zack seemed to turn even more understanding. "Leah, I wouldn't have offered to take you to the inn if I didn't want to be with you. I told you before, I don't pick up girls on the highway. Everything that's happened between us, it's not the norm for me."

"It's not for me, either."

"I know. That's why I brought you by my parents' home. I wanted you to meet them, and for them to meet you. I'm not hiding anything, Leah."

His words made sense. "And here, I thought it was all about those puppies," she said, lightly teasing.

"I hoped you'd go for the puppies. I hoped when you got there, you might feel more comfortable around me."

"I do. I'm not afraid."

For a moment, his gaze warmed. Her breathing quickened. For a moment, his eyes drifted over her face, glanced at her lips.

In that second, she knew he was thinking about kissing her. Instinctively, she knew that she would have let him. There was that strong of a pull between them.

But he didn't. "So, are you ready?"

"I am." She looked in the backseat. "So, I've been meaning to ask, what's in the cooler?"

"Snacks and sandwiches and a couple of bottles of water. My mom's idea. Even though I'm on the highway all day with my work, and could really use a sandwich every now and then, as soon as I tell her I'm traveling across the state line, she starts packing supplies."

"Then we won't go hungry."

Zack buckled up and turned on the ignition. "You're exactly right. No matter what happens, we won't go hungry."

Leah's stomach knotted. It was probably her imagination, but for a moment there, his words sounded extremely ominous.

Chapter 17

Later that evening, Melody spied Levi sitting on the floor with Mary Lundy, Katie and Jonathan's eldest daughter. Around them was a mountain of yarn, all of it twisted and tangled.

"What are you two doing?" she asked as she came to join them.

"Sorting yarn," he replied. "Please join us."

Levi looked so overwhelmed, surrounded by the mountain of string, that Melody couldn't resist his cry for help. Or tease him a bit. "I will . . . if you're sure you don't mind?"

"Please. Have a seat."

"All right." Knowing better than to sit on the floor—if she did that, she wouldn't be able to get up—she sat on a nearby chair and grabbed a fistful of yellow, orange, and green. Strands snaked around and popped out like in a photo of a giant squid she'd seen in a textbook. A few longer pieces continued through to the ball on Mary's lap. "These are tangled horribly! Mary, how did it get this way?"

"Our cat found my *mamm*'s yarn basket and played with it last weekend." With a dramatic grimace, she added, "Katie was terribly upset, I tell ya. She said Patches almost ruined it all."

"Patches sure tried his best," Levi muttered.

Mary ignored him. "As my Christmas gift to her, I offered to sort it."

Melody nodded in her direction seriously. "Perhaps you wouldn't mind if Levi and I stayed for a bit to help?"

"I wouldn't mind, but Katie might get mad. This is my job."

"If she spies us, I'll tell her I offered. Untangling all this yarn is a difficult thing."

"It's awful! I'd throw it all out and go buy new yarn if I could."

"That would be a waste of good money," Levi murmured. "I don't mind sitting here and helping. Do you, Melody?"

His dark eyes flickered her way. Once again inviting her closer. Inviting her to reach out to people. To enjoy the other's company instead of feeling overwhelmed. "I don't mind at all. It will be fun."

Mary snorted. "This ain't fun."

Instead of correcting her surly attitude, Levi just laughed. "There are worse chores to do, I promise you that."

Melody dug through her clump. After pulling apart strands and searching, she uncovered what she was looking for, just like a prize. "I've got the end of the yellow."

"I have the green," Mary offered.

"And I have brown." Levi's eyes twinkled. "The most masculine color."

"It suits you," Melody quipped.

He grinned at her, his expression revealing his surprise. "I didn't know you could joke."

"I might have forgotten, but I do have a sense of humor," she murmured. "There was a time when I used to always tease people around me."

"I used to laugh more, too," Levi said.

In between them, Mary sighed.

Melody glanced at Mary. "Are we boring you, child?"

"No," she said quickly, obviously too polite to speak her mind.

But five minutes later, when her little sister peeked in, the look on Mary's face was priceless. "Hannah, do ya need something?"

"Winnie's going to take me for a walk to gather pinecones. She said you could come."

Glaring at the yarn, she shook her head. However, the rest of her looked wistful. "I best not."

"Why don't you go, Mary?" Levi surprised them by saying. "There're plenty of knots here. They'll be some when you get back still."

She looked from one to the other. "You don't mind?"

"I don't mind at all," Melody said, surprising herself. She was eager to be alone with Levi. Eager to learn more about him, and about how he used to be, without Mary's ears.

"Go now," Levi prodded. "Holidays are for spending time with your family and friends. Go enjoy yourself."

That seemed to be all the encouragement she needed. With a swish of her skirts, she was off and running.

The moment it was just the two of them, Levi stood up with a groan. "Never again let me ever complain about women's work. Sitting here, trying to sort out those strands, is tiring. I need to stretch."

"It is kind of you to even help her as much as you did." She started to move his pile of yarn toward herself.

"Don't—" He reached out and covered her hand with his own, stopping her. When their fingers touched, she stilled.

He pulled his own hand away. "I'm sorry. I didn't mean to grab at you like that."

The proper thing to do would be to pretend nothing had happened. But try as she might, she couldn't. "You have nothing to apologize for. You didn't grab."

"I don't want to frighten you."

If the memories weren't so hard to bear, she would have told him just how different his touch had been from the other man's. "You didn't frighten me. I promise."

Then, because she was learning a bit more about herself . . . and because she knew he was suffering in his own way, she reached out to him. This time, she carefully placed her hand on top of his. Not to caress. Just to still.

But just the same, his hand trembled slightly. It was obvious he, too, didn't know where their boundaries lay.

Quietly, she said, "Ever since I was raped, no one—man or woman—dared touch me. At first I was grateful for it."

"But now?"

"Now I have to admit to missing human contact. Being scared and unsure, it wasn't who I was. It wasn't who I used to be. Deep down, I don't think it's who I am now."

Ever so slowly, he rotated his hand so her palm slowly perched inside of it. "Used to be, I wasn't so stern. I wasn't so judgmental. Far less used to make me frown." He swallowed. "And I never, ever shied away from my wife's touch."

As if their hands belonged to other people, Levi's fingers spread and she slipped her fingers through his. Linking their hands. Heat rushed through her skin, sinking into the fine muscles of her palm. Sinking into her bones.

They were connected.

"I've been meaning to tell you something. Your hand, it feels good in mine," he murmured. She heard a thread of wonder there.

The same wonder she felt. Unable to speak, she nodded.

Just as slowly, their hands loosened. She pulled her hand away. Dug it into the wad of string. "Back to work?"

He pulled up a chair and sat near her. "Back to work," he murmured.

However, he didn't look that upset about it.

Neither was she. In fact, it was so nice sitting with him she could almost ignore the twinges of pain she'd started to feel in her back.

As well as the fact that they seemed to be coming at regular intervals.

Chapter 18

December 24, 1:00 A.M.

Jonathan rolled over and opened one bleary eye. "Katie, is the storm keeping you up?"

As the wind whipped another burst of snow and ice against the windowpane, she shivered. "The storm's bad, but I've been worried about our boy."

She was worried about other things, too. Here in the middle of the night, she'd had so much on her mind. At the forefront was the likelihood that their family would be increasing again—and that Jonathan had no idea.

As the days passed, she knew it was time to tell him about her pregnancy. But there never seemed to be the right time.

Now, in the middle of the night when the rest of the

house was asleep, would be perfect. However, there was a greater issue at hand. Something was wrong with their son.

Eli had become increasingly fussier by the hour. He was feeling warmer, too. Those things, along with a general lack of sleep, had set her nerves on edge. "Nothing I'm doing seems to quiet him. I'm getting worried."

One open eye became two. With a shake of his head, Jonathan sat up. His covers slid down to his waist as he leaned forward and looked her way.

She couldn't help herself from examining him as well. A warmth encased her as she reminded herself once again that this man—this wonderful man—was her husband. Even though so much else was worrying her, Katie felt that same pull toward him that never seemed to go away whenever they were together.

Sometimes, she still could hardly believe they were married and a real couple. The Lord had been so good to her! He'd given her so many blessings. Thinking of her own behavior when Melody and Levi had first arrived, Katie wished she'd remembered then to spend more time giving thanks—instead of resenting their arrival.

A shrill cry from Eli refocused her attention. As best she could, she sought to soothe him, but still his face scrunched up as if in pain. Seconds later, another scream filtered the air.

Jonathan's sleepy expression turned concerned. "When was the last time Eli had Children's Tylenol?"

Katie turned to the glowing clock on her nightstand. The news there made her head pound. "Three hours ago."

"It's, what, one A.M.?"

"*Jah.*" As Eli's fretful squirms threatened to break into louder cries, she bit her lip. Oh, she felt so helpless. She'd give almost everything she had to be able to read her baby's mind. "I don't know what's wrong with him. I don't know what to do." She knew her voice was turning high-pitched and shrill, but she didn't care. "Jonathan, he seems to be in pain, but the bottle's directions are clear. I can only give him medicine every four hours. It's too soon to give him more."

The quilts piled in a heap as he crawled out of bed and padded her way. The long-sleeved T-shirt and plaid flannel pajamas had been her birthday present to him, and never failed to make her feel happy inside. The outfit was a favorite of his, and he often let her know how comfortable it felt.

After he brushed a hand down her back, he held out his arms for their baby. "I'll take a turn."

The moment she handed Eli to him, Jonathan competently tucked him close to his shoulder.

She was thankful for the help, but still worried her lip. Even in Jonathan's solid arms, Eli still squirmed and fussed. "Perhaps it's time to try a bottle?" he asked.

"Maybe. The pressure of swallowing will either lessen the pain or it won't."

As Eli's cries became louder and his little body seemed to go stiff with frustration and pain, Katie knew she had to try anything to help him. "I'll go down to the kitchen and fix a bottle."

"You're tired, Katie. Why don't you try to sleep a bit?"

Jonathan cupped a large hand around the back of her head. "I don't mind taking care of our boy for a bit."

Though exhaustion made her feel like she was dead on her feet, Katie knew she'd never sleep. There was no way she could relax enough to sleep when her baby was so distraught.

Even if she were to lie down, Katie knew she would simply sit in the cold bed and worry about Eli and Jonathan. "I'll go downstairs with you. I won't be able to sleep."

"Katie, I promise he'll be in good hands."

"I sleep better next to you, anyway," she said with a smile and pulled her robe's belt more tightly around her waist. "Besides, Eli's cries are so loud, I'm afraid he's going to wake the rest of the house up."

Instead of saying anything to the contrary, Jonathan simply smiled. "If he hasn't already, I'm sure he's about to. His lungs are working well." Pressing a gentle palm on the small of her back, he guided her forward. "Come on, then. We'll take care of this boy together."

Together, the two of them walked down the dimly lit stairs. Luckily, her mother had invested in a few battery-operated nightlights that were positioned every few feet. Though their dad liked to complain about the expense, her mother—and Anna—had enjoyed the improvement tremendously. It was so nice to be able to walk in the dark without holding a candle or light.

As they continued down, Eli fussing in Jonathan's arms, and Katie stepping right behind them, she said a little prayer of thanks for her husband.

It was times like this that Katie was grateful for their age difference, and for the fact that he'd raised two girls out of their infancy before she'd come into their lives.

Very little rattled her husband. He approached each task with a self-assuredness that made her proud and just a little bit envious, though he often told her that her far more high-strung disposition was a gift for him. For some reason, he enjoyed her energy.

They were a good pair.

When they got to the main floor, Katie darted off to the washroom and pulled out a thick fleece blanket, just in case it was drafty in the kitchen. Then she met Jonathan there. "I'll take him now, if you'll prepare the bottle."

Easily, he passed over the baby. Katie frowned as she felt Eli's too-hot skin. He seemed to shy away from her touch. Fearing he was chilled, she attempted to wrap him up a bit, but he kicked and wiggled against the warmth of the thick blanket.

Obviously, their little journey downstairs didn't ease Eli in the slightest. If anything, he was getting worse. He continued to fuss and cry, stopping only seconds at a time—and that was to inhale.

Jonathan lit the light overhead, then moved to the gas stove. A match lit a burner. Next, he poured some water into a kettle and set it on the flame. When the water got warm, they mixed it with powdered formula and poured it into one of the waiting bottles.

As Eli continued to cry, Katie hoped the water would heat quickly—and that the warm formula would ease the baby's pain.

Usually, Katie liked to nurse the baby herself, but she was glad that her sister Rebekeh had suggested she get Eli used to a bottle, too. Sometimes, Katie was so grateful to give Jonathan a turn holding Eli. He had told her that he enjoyed feeding their baby, too.

Though, it was now unlikely that anything was going to make their cranky boy happy. When he wailed again, Katie bent back her head and sighed. "Oh, Jonathan."

"It's just tears," he murmured gently. "I know you're worried, but we'll soon get him settled."

"I hope you're right." As if in response, Eli arched his back, fisted his palms, and then let out an enormous wail.

Katie resituated him, and rubbed his back. "I hear you, young man," she soothed. "I know you're unhappy. But please, settle down, *jah*? We're doing all we can."

Next to the sink, Jonathan was testing the water's temperature, then pouring a few ounces into a prepared bottle. "This is almost ready."

"Is there anything I can do?" Melody stood at the doorway, wrapped in a thick robe and wool socks. She looked bleary-eyed.

Katie knew their trip downstairs had woken her up. Years of duty assailed her, making her feel guilty. It was almost as if she could hear her mother's voice chiding her from behind.

Guests came to the inn to relax, not to be disturbed.

But before she could apologize, Katie spied something familiar in the girl's gaze. A desire to not be alone.

Melody stepped forward. "I'm happy to help, if I can."

Katie felt humbled. Once again Melody was reaching

out for others, pushing her own needs to one side. "I thank you for the offer, but there's not much you can do. We're fine."

"Well, we are as fine as we can be, what with a screaming sick baby to make happy," Jonathan corrected as he handed the bottle to Katie. "But you're welcome to join us, if you'd like."

Katie took the bottle and placed it in Eli's mouth. She held her breath as he took a tentative taste, then sucked the bottle some more.

The quiet that blanketed them all felt like the best gift in the world.

"Peace at last," Jonathan murmured.

"Melody, I am sorry we woke you," Katie said when she could finally bear to look anywhere but at the baby.

"Please don't worry. I think the winds outside are louder than Eli. I have a hard time sleeping, anyway. I've been, ah, restless tonight. It sounds foolish, but I was pleased to have an excuse to walk around." Little by little, Melody stepped into the room, and then finally slipped into one of the chairs.

"I had a hard time sleeping when my time to deliver was so close."

Melody smiled. "Really? That makes me feel better. All the books talk about sleeping as much as possible because I'll need that sleep when the baby's born. But I can't seem to get comfortable."

"I don't know any woman who could get comfortable with a bowling ball rolling around her middle." Katie smiled as Jonathan started to look like he would rather be anywhere than there in the kitchen, discussing pregnancy issues. "Jon, why don't you go back to bed?"

"I don't want to leave you."

"Look, Eli's eyes are finally closing. We might all get some sleep soon. Go on up," she said again. "I'll follow you in a few moments."

With a weary smile, he nodded. "I won't argue about that." After pressing his lips to her head, he nodded in Melody's direction. *"Gud naught."*

She raised a hand. "Good night." When they were alone, Melody blushed. "I am sorry I intruded. I really did hope I could help."

"Please don't worry. My nerves are so strained, I wouldn't have been able to sleep this minute, anyway. He was really crying. Actually, I'm kind of surprised we don't have the whole house in here."

Melody gestured toward the oven. "Would you like some tea? I see there's a dish of chamomile here by the stove."

"That would be very kind of you. Thank you."

"Don't get up. I can work a stove just fine," said Melody.

Moments later, Eli's mouth went slack and his hand loosened. Wearily, Katie ran a hand along his scalp. To her relief, his temperature seemed a bit cooler. Perhaps it was all his crying and not a sickness that had gotten him so heated up.

In no time at all, Melody was back, holding two mugs of piping hot tea. The tantalizing aroma of chamomile beckoned Katie; and now that she could put the bottle down, she sipped gratefully.

Across from her, Melody sipped, too. She looked so pleased to not be alone that, once again, Katie worried about the girl. Pregnancy and babies were hard enough with a kind, competent man like Jonathan at her side. In addition, Katie also had her mother's guidance and her best friend Anna's support.

So far, she hadn't read a single book about pregnancy or caring for an infant. There hadn't been any need—she had a wealth of knowledge all around her.

But the opposite seemed to be the case for Melody. If she was here alone, she must not have a lot of family members to offer her guidance and support.

"So, are you going to keep your baby or give it up for adoption?"

Melody stared at Katie and felt a lump form in her throat. The question had been honestly asked, without rancor. Simple curiosity. So different from most everyone else she knew, who were determined to relay to her what they thought she should do and why. "I'd like to keep it."

"You would like to?" Katie tilted her head to one side. "I'm sorry, but the way you are phrasing that makes me think you're not sure you can."

"That's because I'm not. Babies are expensive." For a moment, Melody paused. She didn't like admitting her flaws, her weaknesses. But she didn't want to sound like the type of woman who didn't make plans, either. "The fact is, I don't have much money."

Katie sipped her tea. In her arms, little Eli breathed deeply, his mouth half open. His easy limpness looked

almost comical after his tense exertions just a few moments ago. "Babies do seem to cost more than I imagined,"
she finally said. "What about your parents? Will they help
you financially?"

"I don't know what they want to do." Melody felt her
cheeks heating. Even to her own ears, her answers sounded
mysteriously vague. But the problem was that she didn't
have any answers. She didn't know what she was going to
do in her future.

She'd been so worried about coming to grips with the
attack, she'd neglected to hope much for the future.

"Can't you talk to them?"

"Not like I used to. Sometimes I feel like my parents
and I could be close—if this baby would just go away.
Sometimes, I think perhaps that would be best. That the
right thing to do would be to give this baby to a couple.
A husband and wife who lived far away from me. Who
would always look at this child as a gift—not a reminder
of something painful."

"Do you think that's how you are going to be? That
you'll never be able to look beyond how it was conceived?"

"I don't know. I'd like to think that wouldn't be me.
But I'm not positive." She sighed. "All I do know is that if I
wasn't pregnant, if I wasn't about to have a newborn, then
I could go back to how things used to be."

"You never will, you know."

Melody started. Katie's voice was flat. Honest. Almost
as if she knew about heartbreak. "I think you're probably
right."

"Yes." Katie's words were a statement. Not a question.

"Since I've been here, I've been wondering why my parents didn't put up much of a fuss when I told them I was coming here. They were surprised, but they didn't try to persuade me otherwise." She shrugged. For nine months' time, she'd been lying to herself about their natures. But here, in the safety of the Brennemans' kitchen, she was suddenly too tired to begin the lies again. "More likely, I think they were relieved."

"You have no one? No beau?"

"After this? Not likely."

Katie hesitated, then murmured, "Not every man is cruel and violent, Melody."

"I know that. But the men I know don't seem to know what to make of me." Because she didn't want to sound quite so pitiful, she said, "I do have an English friend named Leah. We're close."

"I'm glad."

"She was disappointed that I was coming here, but she said maybe it was what I needed."

"She sounds smart." Katie sipped her tea once more, then stood up with a yawn. "My Jonathan will wonder what happened to me if I don't get to sleep. I'll regret it tomorrow, as well. The clock keeps ticking, you know."

Melody took the mugs, threw away the teabags, and rinsed them out. "Thank you for staying here to talk to me."

"No, thank you for offering your help. It was nice of you."

"But you didn't need anything."

"You reached out to me. That, I needed; I'm grateful. Good night, Melody. I'll save you some muffins, so please try and sleep late."

"I might just do that," Melody said as Katie headed upstairs.

Alone now in the kitchen, she made sure the flame on the range was extinguished, then turned off the overhead light. In the dark, she walked down the short hallway to her own room and crawled under the covers as best she could.

Another wave of cramps flew through her stomach, but they weren't too bad.

Chapter 19

December 24, 3:00 A.M.

"I can't believe I brought you out in this storm," Leah told Zack wearily as they watched the snow swirl onto the highway from the fast food restaurant they had taken shelter in. "Every mile seems worse than the last. The roads are really treacherous."

"They're bad, but I've been on worse. It's just snow."

Leah was slowly coming to realize that very little seemed to upset Zack Littleton. The whole time, his manner had been relaxed and easygoing.

She, of course, was anxious enough for the both of them. And was starting to feel guilty about the journey he was accompanying her on. "But it's a lot of snow. We should have arrived at the Brennemans' hours ago. Now I don't even think we're going to make it to a hotel tonight. I'm so sorry."

He raised a brow. "Why are you apologizing? You can't control the weather."

"You know what I mean."

Reaching out, he took her hand and pressed it between his palms. "Please don't worry so much. I'm fine, and so are you. We'll get there."

"This isn't what you signed up for."

Zack's lips twitched. "How do you know that I didn't sign up for this?"

"What do you mean?"

"Leah, don't you get it? The only reason I volunteered to take you is because I wanted to spend time with you."

The warm feelings that he gave her challenged the confusion she was experiencing. "But . . . I thought you felt sorry for Melody?"

"I do. I feel very sorry for her. But I don't know her." Gently, he squeezed her palm. "I do know you. And I wanted to get to know you more. This trip is allowing me to do that."

"For better or worse," she grumbled. And, she had been on the "worse" side for quite a while now. All she'd been doing was worrying and fussing and complaining. "I'll try not to make you crazy with my worries."

"Worry all you want. I can take it." Before she could reply to that, he looked out the window again and frowned. "Besides, if we're going to start blaming people, we'd have to blame me. If I hadn't insisted that we needed to stop to help those women on I-275, we might have gotten a whole lot farther."

"But that isn't you." In her heart, she knew that. Even though he worked for the state of Kentucky and not Ohio, none of that seemed to make a difference when he saw someone in need.

Zack looked intrigued by her statement. "It's not, huh?" Something warm and inviting entered his eyes—making her want to be closer to him. "So, do you already know me that well?"

"Maybe. Well, I *want* to know you that well." She smiled, enjoying their light flirtation—as they'd been flirting for quite some time now. "I know you're the kind of man who helps girls in traffic accidents."

"That's my job."

". . . And who doesn't mind taking me to a movie on a snowy day. And who likes puppies, and people you meet on the side of the road."

He winked. "Only redheads."

"I know you don't mind doing dishes."

"My mother would have killed me if I hadn't washed dishes."

"I know you are the kind of guy who offers to drive complete strangers to see a friend."

"You're not a complete stranger." He dropped her hand as he leaned a little bit closer. "You've never seemed like a stranger to me. From the moment I first talked to you on the side of the road, there was something special about you that caught my attention."

"I . . . I felt the same way."

"In fact, I feel like we've gone from strangers to acquaintances to friends to maybe even something more." He swallowed. "I mean, we're getting to know each other really well."

She couldn't deny it. And wasn't even sure if she wanted to. "Perhaps."

His eyes sparkled. "Ah-hah! Caught you. You have to admit we're not strangers."

A lump felt like lead in her belly. No, that wasn't how she was feeling about him at all. Fact was, she was falling hard for Office Zack Littleton, and she didn't fall hard for anyone. He was like her perfect catalog guy. Handsome and tall. He was patient and had a sense of humor. And he was kind to everyone. Puppies, old ladies, his mom.

And yet . . . he didn't seem like a marshmallow, either. Back at a gas station, he'd held his own against a couple of guys who were giving the cashier a hard time.

She trusted him. Completely. So completely, it didn't even make sense, not rationally. The fact was, she felt more at ease with this man than with some men she'd dated in the past months. What did that mean? Did things like this really happen? This . . . instant infatuation?

What was worse, she didn't even care. All she wanted to do was be around him. And hold his hand.

Because just a few miles back, they'd started holding hands in the truck and it had been nice.

"You're right. We're not strangers at all. I guess we're closer to friends."

"I think so."

As she continued to reflect how nice it was to be with him, to hold his hand, a sudden, awful thought floated forward. "Hey—you don't have a girlfriend, do you?"

He looked horrified. "Do you really think I'd be asking you to stay in Louisville . . . asking you to spend so much time with me if I did?"

"I . . . I don't think so."

"Leah, I promise you, there's no other girl in my life."

"I find that hard to believe."

"I had a girlfriend a year ago. We broke up. I'll tell you about it sometime. But I want you to know that I haven't been looking for anyone. Hadn't even really been thinking about it, until I saw you."

"I'm not dating anyone, either."

He folded his arms across his chest. "I hope not. I mean, I did show you Trixie's pups."

Pleased the mood was lighter, and that he'd told her more about himself, she teased right back. "It's only because of those puppies that I trusted you enough to drive me around."

"Leah." His voice was softer now, gentle. He drew out her name sweetly, giving her goose bumps. "I don't want to scare you, but I promise, you're special to me. I'd never hurt you."

"Well, I hoped you wouldn't. I'm sorry, Zack. I want to trust you, but I'm afraid, you know?"

"I know." Softly, he said, "Years ago, I got my heart broken, too."

She stared at him in surprise. "How did you know that happened to me?"

"I noticed the signs." Standing up, he held out his hand to help her hop off the stool. "I think we should get on our way again."

She zipped up her coat and followed him outside. It felt completely natural when he wrapped an arm around her waist and walked by her side. Ready to catch her in case she slipped.

And then, when they reached the passenger side door, he wrapped his other arm around her and drew her to him.

There, in the dark—with the snow coming down and layer upon layer of down coats between them—they hugged.

She felt his lips press against her brow. "Leah, you've got to know that I'm falling for you. I like you a lot."

As she felt his lips brush her brow again, she exhaled and snuggled closer. Taking a chance, she lifted her chin and stared into his eyes. Pure happiness reflected in them. Very slowly, he brushed his lips against hers in a sweet kiss. Then he stepped back and opened the door for her.

Sliding into the cab, Leah knew what was happening between them was a once in a lifetime thing. The man was special; she liked him. But what she really liked was how open he was. He was offering himself in such a generous, easy way. No games or lies.

And he was patient with her, too. From the moment he'd asked if she would wait to be rescued by the tow truck, Leah had known that he would have immediately backed off at any time she wanted to.

During their whole trip, he'd been letting her set the

pace, she realized in surprise. He'd offered suggestions, but had let all the decision making fall to her.

As the silence in the cab lengthened, he relaxed his grip on her hand, and noticeably gripped his steering wheel harder. Waiting.

"I like you, too, Zack. Actually, I like you a lot. I would hate it if this was all one-sided."

"I promise, it's not. Already, I want to make plans for this weekend and next and the week after that."

"Really?"

"Really. Leah, for the last hour, I've been sitting here, trying to figure out a way to ask you the same thing. You know, ask if I can come visit you again."

"You shouldn't have been worried."

"Why is that?"

"Oh, because I am seeing someone. But he's a nice guy."

"What?"

He looked so stricken, so bummed, she couldn't tease him any longer. "My boyfriend's name is Zack Littleton. He works for the state highway patrol and lives in Louisville, Kentucky. And just for the record, he's a really nice guy. I can't imagine what my life would be if he hadn't stepped into it."

"I can't imagine, either." When she reached for his hand, he took it, curving his fingers around her own as if they were the most precious thing he had held.

After a moment, Zack very gently, very carefully, brought her knuckles to his lips. He barely kissed them, but the sensation caused a buzz of awareness through her body. Leah had shared far more intimate kisses that had affected her not near as much.

"Hearing what you said, it made my day."

Leah looked at their joined fingers. Thought about how comforted she felt. How safe and special.

Oh, she felt so lucky. "When you say things like that, I hardly mind the snow at all."

She knew God had pulled them together. She knew he was watching them from afar, guiding them, watching over them.

Oh, at that moment, she felt like the luckiest woman in the world. Right there, in a snowstorm in the middle of the night.

On Christmas Eve.

Chapter 20

December 24, 10:00 A.M.

Melody was in labor. A few hours after she'd told Katie good night and fell asleep, the pains had intensified. Now she knew without a doubt that she'd been experiencing labor pains for quite a while.

She'd been pacing the room, trying to pretend the pains were going to vanish soon, when her water broke. Now she knew she had no choice but to face reality. She was going to have a baby soon, and she was going to have to tell the Brennemans.

As she walked to the kitchen, another band of pain gripped her hard. Closing her eyes, Melody leaned against the wall and breathed slowly. She had learned that the pain eased somewhat if she didn't fight it so much.

As soon as the contraction subsided, she opened her

eyes . . . and found Levi by her side. "I was walking by when I saw you standing here," he said by way of explanation. "Melody, are you all right?"

"As well as I can be. The baby is on its way." She exhaled as the pain dissipated.

Concern and relief flashed across his features, then were replaced by sheer horror. "We need to get you out of here. You must go to the hospital."

"I don't know if that's possible. The storm is fierce outside."

"Perhaps it's not that bad."

She almost smiled when an answering knock of wind slammed against the windows. The winter storm had arrived with a vengeance, and seemed certain to hold them hostage. "I think it is."

Tenderly, he brushed the back of two fingers along her cheek. "Let's hope not."

She felt strengthened by his touch. By his concern. So glad he hadn't shied away, she said, "This sounds strange, but I'm glad you're at the inn, too. I feel better when you're nearby."

For a moment, Levi looked ready to run—ready to escape—but then some inner resolve rushed through him. "If you need me, then of course I'll be here for you."

"*Danke.*"

"All right, then. Let's go tell everyone else." He wrapped a reassuring arm around her shoulders and led her into the kitchen. "Everyone, Melody here is going to have a baby." His words were jerky. Stilted.

Melody almost smiled. She knew he was *naerfich*—

nervous. She knew her being in labor brought back difficult memories. But here he was, doing the best he could.

He really was a kind man, she thought . . . just as another contraction came.

From across the room, Katie watched Melody's eyes close in pain and felt her stomach sink to the floor. "Melody?" she cried out. "When did everything start? Just a few hours ago you seemed fine."

"I've been trying to ignore the pains, I'm afraid." Visibly shaken, Melody licked her lips and tried again. "I don't think they're going to stop."

"Then I guess you'll be havin' a baby here," her mother said matter-of-factly.

Turning to her mother, Katie silently pleaded for her to take charge. *"Mamm?"*

But her mother had already rushed forward. "I think we will need to get you settled into bed, dear," she told Melody as she pulled her from Levi's side and guided her to the hall. "It's going to be a long day."

Without a word, Levi turned on his heel and left.

Leaving Katie to stare at Anna and Winnie. "This makes me a nervous wreck," Katie confided. "I don't know anyone besides Rebekeh who's had a baby at home recently. And she, of course, can't be here because she can't travel for hours in the bad weather."

"We'll get through it," Winnie said as optimistic as ever. "I mean, Melody will."

"Perhaps we could get to the hospital, somehow? It is light now . . ."

"Have you looked outside, Katie? It's sleeting and snowing. We can't take a horse out in this. They'll break their legs."

"Perhaps the ambulance? We should call."

"The phone lines are down," Anna said quietly. "Henry said most likely the weight of the ice pulled them down. I'm afraid we're on our own."

Winnie reached out and grasped her hand. "Katie, what is wrong?"

"I don't know. I feel so helpless. I feel like we should be doing everything we can for that poor girl and we're not."

"There's nothing wrong with worrying, but that's not what she needs right now. We need to think positively. Altogether, we'll be able to help Melody, *jah*? Our families are wonderful-*gut* at helping each other out in difficult situations." After giving Katie another reassuring hug, Winnie took her hand. "Come, now. Let's go see what your mother needs from us."

Holding hands, they walked into Melody's room and saw her *mamm* standing by the girl's side, looking as calm and serene as ever. Seeing her mother's expression, remembering how nervous and excited she'd been—and most of all, recalling how Jonathan's tenderness had made Eli's birth one of the most perfect moments of her life—Katie pulled herself together.

Her mother looked at her with a new respect. "Katie, sit with Melody for a bit, would ya? Winnie, I'm going to need your help to get sheets and such."

"Of course," Katie said as Winnie and her mother left the room. Pasting a smile on her face, she rushed forward.

"Oh, Melody, just think, soon you'll be holding your babe."

"I'm scared."

"I know, but you have to relax," she murmured, remembering just how she'd felt when she had been in labor with Eli. "It's time to be brave, yes?"

Slowly, Melody nodded. "*Jah.* I'll try."

Katie was just about to ask if Melody had any questions when Jonathan appeared at the door. His face was as pale as she'd ever seen it. "Jonathan?"

He didn't spare a look Melody's way. "It's Eli, Katie."

"What . . . what's wrong?"

"He's not breathing too well. His fever's spiked again, and he's all wheezy and barky."

"Barky?" She'd never heard of such a term.

"Your father thinks he has the croup," he said, his voice urgent. "He's holding him now . . . but we need you."

With the door wide open, Katie could hear Eli's wail. Every feeling within pushed her to leave that very second.

But duty called, too. This woman, a girl really, was about to give birth. And she was completely alone. So alone that she'd traveled to their inn for Christmas. How could she leave her? Katie bit her lip as she turned to the girl.

But before she could think of anything to say, Melody motioned her away. "Go. Eli needs you."

"I'll just go check on him for a moment. I'll be back—"

"I'll be fine."

Katie edged away. "My *mamm* will be in soon."

Melody nodded, opened her mouth, hesitated for a moment, then blurted, "Katie, would you see if maybe Levi could sit in here with me for a spell?"

Katie tried to hide her surprise. Rarely did men visit a birthing room. And never had she heard of a man visiting who wasn't a husband.

But, perhaps, in a strange way it all made sense. These were unusual circumstances. "Of course. I'll go get him now."

She rushed out of the room to find Anna heating a bottle for Eli. By her side were Hannah and Mary, each looking more scared than the other. *"Mamm!"* Hannah cried. "Our baby is sick."

"I know. Where is he?"

"Daed took Eli up to the shower. He said sometimes the steam helps," Mary supplied.

"Anna, could you bring that up when it's ready?"

"I'll send it with Mary and then go sit with Melody. She shouldn't be alone."

Katie halted. "Oh, I almost forgot. She asked for Levi. Where is he?"

"I'll find him for you," Anna said. "Now, go on. Go to your baby."

Katie didn't wait another moment.

Chapter 21

December 24, 11:00 A.M.

"Levi, thank heavens I found you," Anna said as soon as she entered the hearth room.

When the storm had gotten worse, Levi had donned gloves and gone outside to help Henry and Sam carry in more wood. He'd been more than happy to do the chore. He was eager to be as busy as possible so he wouldn't think about Melody being in labor . . . or stew on memories of Christmases past. "I've been out in the barn with your husband. Chopping wood."

"Levi, Melody asked for you."

Everything inside of him stilled. "But she's in labor."

"I know that. However, she asked for you."

He shook his head. *Please God*, he prayed. *Please don't ask this of me*. "I wouldn't be much good in there."

"But she asked for you."

"Anna, I cannot."

Eyes blazing, she marched forward, giving him the first glimpse of how she must have been in her former life, when she was English. "I don't care who or what you think she needs. The fact of the matter is she has asked for you. Go in there and sit with her."

Images of Rosanna crying as the pains got unbearable flashed in his head. Of him sitting by her side, completely helpless. Of the blood. Of the loss. "You don't understand—"

Right before his eyes, Anna's temper broke. "Levi Bender, you listen to me. There. Is. No. One. Else. My nephew is terribly sick. My father-in-law, Jonathan, and Katie are with him. Henry has to now take care of the animals. My two nieces are in their rooms crying, and Winnie has her hands full with them. Finally, my mother and I are trying to get the phone to work and prepare the house. Besides . . . *Melody asked for you*."

"Anna, if I could . . ."

She gripped his hand so hard, he felt indentations from her short nails dig into his skin. "I promise you, you can. I believe in you." More quietly, she added, "And God does, too." Looking completely exasperated, she looked up to him. "Please don't think you came here to the inn by chance. Our Lord wanted you here for a reason. Perhaps it is for Melody? Perhaps it is for yourself? Now, go. Please, Levi. Please."

He knew she was right. "All right. I'll go now."

She sighed in relief. "Melody's still in her room," Anna murmured before darting away.

Feeling like a sleepwalker, Levi left the hearth room and crossed into the kitchen. All the time, he thought about Anna's remarks.

Thought about the Lord and His wishes. And his earlier conversation with Mr. Brenneman.

For so long, he'd pushed God away. He had never understood why Rosanna had to die. He'd never understood why she'd had to suffer so much.

Perhaps when he arrived in heaven and talked with the Lord, he'd learn the reasons. But for now, he followed Anna's words and shook off the last of his doubts and burdens.

When he stepped through the corridor to Melody's room, he felt as composed and in control as he'd ever been.

Both Mrs. Brenneman and Melody looked up when he entered the room. Mrs. Brenneman's face showed relief.

But all he really could see was Melody. Slowly, her lips curved as he approached her bedside. "You're here."

"I am." Sitting down in the chair the innkeeper had just vacated, he reached for her hand. Held it gently between his own. "I'm here, and I won't leave you."

The smile she gave him was so full of hope, so sincere, so strong in her belief in him, that it took his breath away. God was with them—His presence so strong that Levi felt it as a tangible thing.

Everything, somehow, was going to be all right.

* * *

December 24, 3:00 P.M.

"Are we there yet?" Leah asked Zack, in a dumb attempt to lighten the mood.

"I wish. The visibility is really getting bad out here."

She looked at the glowing Garmin he had attached to his windshield. By its estimation, they would arrive at the inn within the hour; but it had been indicating that for the last two. A little surge of nervousness fluttered in her stomach again. Through their whole journey, Officer Zack Littleton had displayed nothing but relaxed ease. Very little on the road seemed to faze him.

But over the last hour, he seemed to be getting more and more tense. "Is there anything I can do?"

Hardly daring to do more than glance her way, he shook his head. "No, I'm just ready to get there. You know?"

"Yes." His voice was clipped; something was definitely bothering him. "Are you upset with me?"

"Why would I be upset?"

"Because somehow you got involved in this interminable drive."

Zack smiled at that. "If anything, I'm relieved that you found me. I would've been worried sick about you. I'm really glad you let me come with you."

"Glad? Well, that's one way of putting it."

"Let's talk about something else. When can I see you again?"

Though she knew he had changed the topic to relieve their stress, Leah couldn't help but feel a burst of hope. "Whenever you want."

"Let's make plans. What are you doing for New Year's?" There was a smile in his voice.

"Actually, I don't have plans yet."

"Then maybe you can make plans with me?"

She was just about to tell him that she'd love to do that when his Garmin beeped. She looked at the map while the musical voice directed Zack to turn right in 1.2 miles.

"Oh, thank you for that," he said. "We must finally be close."

"You're really anxious, aren't you?"

"It's more than that," he said slowly. "The fact is, we're running low on gas and it's pretty much a certainty that there won't be a gas station anywhere for miles."

"Especially one that's open on Christmas Eve," Leah finished.

As the Garmin sent out another notice, and Zack complied, turning right then sliding a bit as he righted himself, Leah checked the ETA again.

Yet again, it said they were due to arrive in one hour.

The knot in her stomach intensified.

Chapter 22

December 24, 5:00 P.M.

If Melody had any of the books the counselor had given her about labor and delivery on hand, she knew she would have tried to set them on fire.

Nowhere had she read about how incredibly long the birthing process would be. She was fairly certain they'd sugarcoated the pain as well.

As the extreme discomfort of yet another contraction made her mind hazy, she vaguely recalled something about women asking for pain medication. Of course none of that was at the bed-and-breakfast, even if she wanted such a thing.

As the latest cramp faded, she became aware once again

of Levi sitting next to her. He'd been with her now for three hours—at her request.

His face was grave with worry as he studied hers. "Another bad one?"

They were all bad, but she couldn't tell him that. Levi was fighting his own distress and demons just by being in the room with her. "It wasn't too terrible," she lied. "Have I told you that your presence makes it all more bearable?"

For the first time in hours, his expression softened. "Not in the last five minutes. I'm glad I can help." His eyes clouded again. "Though, in truth, I'm not doing anything."

The fact that he was there was enough. "You are," she said simply.

Her door was closed for privacy. Every so often, Mrs. Brenneman came in, but her visits weren't much of a comfort. The innkeeper was terribly worried. Her grandson's breathing was still labored, and Katie was worried sick. In addition, their phone line was still out, so there was no way to call for help for any of them.

Taking a horse and buggy out into the frigid weather when the sky was so dark was foolhardy, too. Especially on Christmas Eve.

Christmas Eve!

How easy it was to forget that such a momentous day was upon them. And how easy it was to imagine how lost and alone Mary must have felt.

As if her body had needed the reminder, another pain gripped her tight.

Levi leaned forward and wrapped an arm around her

shoulders as she sat upright. "Easy now, Melody. Let the pain run its course. It's easier if you don't fight it."

"Like you would know," she snapped.

He had the nerve to grin. "Ah, I wondered if you'd ever get cross."

"It hurts, Levi."

"I know. But just breathe easy, yes?"

As the pain eased away, she relaxed against him. He rubbed her shoulders. "Better?" he murmured.

"Yes. *Danke*." When she turned her head to meet his gaze, he blushed.

Quickly, he dropped his hand. "I'm sorry. I wasn't thinking. I had hoped the support would help . . ."

"Levi, it did. I was glad for it."

"Good."

Melody felt a twinge of regret. He had to be tired. The right thing would be to let him leave . . . to swallow her fears and allow him his freedom. She would be all right. Surely, Mrs. Brenneman would come in again soon.

"Melody, do you think you'll ever love?"

The question was as startling as his voice. It was cool, reserved.

"Why do you ask?"

In the dim light, a band of red stained his cheeks. "Because of what happened . . ."

"Perhaps . . . I don't know. Why?"

To her dismay, his eyes widened.

"No reason."

Grateful to think about anything besides her labor

pains, she said, "I've never been in love. But . . . when I look at the couples here, at Katie and Jonathan and their concern for each other . . . at Sam and Winnie, and the joy they seem to have in each other's company . . . at Henry and Anna"—her breath hitched—"Henry looks at his wife like he would do anything for her. *Anything at all.* Even imagining a man half as in love with me is tempting."

"They all do seem happy together."

Right on time, another contraction gripped her hard. Levi wrapped his arm around her again, coaxing her, supporting her, and then moved away when it passed.

He looked at the clock on the bedside table. "Six minutes apart. They're getting closer."

"I don't know if I'm happy about that or not," she said with a smile.

"Might as well be happy, yes?"

His voice, so caring and sure, gave her confidence— maybe even enough to tell him more, to tell him things she'd told no one besides the doctor and counselors. "Levi, when I was raped . . ."

"Yes?"

Staring off into space, she forced herself to speak. To return to that day. That twenty minutes. "I, um, never know how much to tell people. How much they want to hear."

He kept his voice low. Quiet. So quiet. "I want to hear whatever you want to say."

"Levi, the truth is, I . . . I didn't struggle much. At first, what he was doing, was so surprising, so foreign to me, I was stunned. And then, when I fell to the ground . . ."

"To the ground . . ." he echoed, his voice thick.

"I hit my head on the pavement. Hard." She closed her eyes, trying to remember, praying that she wouldn't. "Levi, still, sometimes, I feel that the whole thing happened to someone else. Later, they told me I had a concussion."

"Because you hurt your head."

"Badly. The fact of the matter, is that I was in a daze, unconscious—for much of the time." She closed her eyes in shame. Hearing her story out loud, it sounded so terrible. Why hadn't she fought more? How was it possible that she didn't remember more?

Worse, how could it be that she'd come to terms with that?

As her words hung in the air between them, as her body prepared itself for another contraction, Melody mentally prepared herself for his rejection. After all, who would want to know her if they found out the truth?

But instead of standing up and walking away, Levi reached out and gripped her hand. "I'm glad," he blurted. "I mean, I'm glad you were unconscious. I mean . . . what happened, I don't want you to remember it. I would never wish you more pain."

As the contraction rolled through, she studied his face. He looked miserable. His obvious regret about not having the right words touched her heart.

When she could breathe easily again, she finished her story. "My parents, they're not bad people, but what happened took them off guard, you know? It created a wedge between us."

"I'm sorry."

"But, even though there was that barrier, they did try to help. They met me at the hospital as soon as they could. And when the doctor and nurse told them that I needed to talk to a professional, they encouraged me to speak to a counselor."

"That is a rare thing. Many parents in our community would distrust outsiders' opinions."

"I'll always be grateful for that. The counselor helped me so much. I visited her for several months. So, I guess what I'm trying to say, is I thank God that I wasn't hurt worse."

He swallowed hard. "I can't imagine being able to give thanks for any of that."

"We have to, don't you think? He gives us opportunities to count our blessings every day, even when the world seems darkest. He gives us sun and snow and hope."

After a moment, a new understanding entered his expression. "Yes, he does, at that. Even for men who've lost their wives . . . for men who are filled with doubts and regrets, he gives us Grace."

She laughed softly. "Yes, Grace is a wonderful, powerful gift."

Holding her hand between his own, he said, "Melody, when this is all over, when we go home again, I'd like to stay in touch with you."

Melody wanted to see him again, too. But she wanted to be sure of his reasons. Was he simply overcome by pity for her? "Why?"

"Because I want to get to know you better. Because I know you'll be on my mind."

"I would like that." Instinctively, she knew that Levi wasn't used to sharing much. He wasn't used to putting his wishes out, for anyone to see.

He leaned closer then. Rubbed a thumb across her knuckles. His face, so beautifully earnest, looked as if he had his whole heart to tell her. "Melody—"

She breathed deeply. Not thinking about anything but his expression, about the wonder of what was happening between them. "Yes?"

"Melody, I want you to know—"

She gasped as the bedroom door slammed open. Levi jumped back. Melody tried to hold her composure as another contraction coursed through her body—and her best friend in the world barreled into the room looking like an avenging angel. "Melody! *Oh*, Melody. I can't believe I found you!"

"Leah?" Melody was so surprised, so overtaken by the next contraction, so stunned by what had just happened between herself and Levi, she could only stare in wonder.

And struggle to breathe as the pain came again.

Chapter 23

December 24, 6:00 P.M.

"I don't know what else to do, Jonathan," Katie said as she stared down at their baby boy. "The steam doesn't seem to be working." For the last thirty minutes, they'd sat together next to the shower going full blast, sending hot air and steam into the room—hoping against hope that the vapors would open little Eli's breathing passages.

But still it looked like he was struggling.

"It might be. He sounds a bit better." Sitting beside her on the edge of the bathtub, Jonathan carefully reached over and smoothed one finger along the baby's head. Little Eli stared up at him in wonder, his dark blue eyes an exact replica of Katie's.

While it was true that Eli was no longer making that

horrible barking sound, his breath was still labored. Slowly, she dared to whisper the worst. "What if it's gotten worse? What if his chest is so tight with sickness that he can't cough any longer?"

"Don't say that."

She closed her eyes in frustration. That was Jonathan's way, of course. He'd been through so much . . . his wife's death, his barn burning, struggling to raise two girls alone. He refused to borrow trouble.

But Katie knew from experience that fearing the worst wasn't always borrowing trouble. Sometimes it helped a person prepare for bad things. "Jonathan, we need to consider taking him to the hospital."

His eyes flashed a refusal. That was easy to see, even in the hot, steamy bathroom. "How do you think we're going to manage that? Taking him around in the buggy in the snow? In the cold?"

"We might not have a choice," she murmured as Eli's body squirmed and he let out a cry. "I can't lose him."

"Don't talk like that." His voice was hard and diffident. It brooked no disagreement.

It was so unlike his usual, gentle manner that it caught her off guard. But even his anger didn't curb her tongue. "We must be prepared, Jonathan."

For a moment, the only sound between them was the rush of water as it hit the porcelain floor. "I know," he said finally. Then, grudgingly, he spoke again. "Katie, it's not just Eli's health that I'm worried about."

"Who else?"

"I'm worried about yours, of course."

"What are you talking about? I feel fine."

Staring at her quietly, he murmured, "Katie, I know you're with child. When were you going to tell me?"

He knew about her pregnancy. Shock followed by despair flowed through her as she stared right back. Oh, was he mad? Disappointed in her?

Why in the world had she waited so long to tell him, anyway?

"I—I didn't know how to tell you that our life was about to get even more hectic," she stammered. "How did you know?"

Carefully, he brushed a tendril of hair from her forehead. "I'm your husband, Katie. I notice everything about you. I notice when you are tired." His gaze warmed. "I know when you are sick . . . and with child. I recognized the signs. I wish you would have told me."

"I didn't know how."

"It's an easy enough thing to say, don't you think?"

"It wasn't that. Jonathan, I was upset about it."

"You don't want another child?"

"I do, but I wasn't ready to have one so soon." Feeling utterly hopeless, she said, "Some days, I feel like I can hardly handle Mary and Hannah and Eli! I don't know how I'm going to handle one more. I don't want to disappoint you." Finally, she dared to confess the awful truth. "I don't want you to wish I was a better wife."

"My *Liewi*," he murmured, wrapping his arms around her. "Don't you know by now that your trials are mine, too? I'll help you. I promise, I will help."

"But I should be able to do everything."

"There's a reason the Lord gave us to each other. He knows you need me, and He also knows that I want to be needed. Lean on me, Katie. Let me bear the weight of your burdens."

Oh, she'd been so wrong not to trust him, and not to trust his love for her. "I'll try."

"Promise?"

"I promise."

His hands fell away as Eli suddenly coughed. "Oh, Eli." With a look of despair, he held a hand out toward the water raining down from the faucet. His fingers laced within the stream. One second. Two. "It's cooling."

Looking down at their boy, Katie felt as if her heart was going to burst. This baby was her heart. From the moment she'd discovered she was pregnant, she'd done everything in her power to be a good mother to him. And now as his eyes drifted closed, but his breathing became labored once again, she realized that even her best might not ever be enough.

He was in the Lord's hands. "Jesus," she whispered, "your birth was a miracle. Your life and teachings have amazed us all. Please be with us tonight. Please watch over Eli. Please heal him with your spirit. He's so little, so dear . . . just as you were once, too. I'm giving my burdens to you, in your name. Amen."

Next to her, Jonathan turned off the water and stood up. Then, as he helped her to her feet, he wrapped an arm around her and guided the three of them to their room.

Katie paused by the bassinet. "I can't bear to put him there."

"Then set him in bed, in between us. And perhaps, we'll sleep, too."

"We can't sleep. There's so much to do . . ."

"Katie, you were up most of last night. I was, too. Let's try, *jah*?" Pressing his lips to her brow, he murmured, "Your prayer was so right, Katie. I'm sure the Lord heard us. We need some rest."

"I am so tired," she admitted. Already her eyelids felt weighted.

"I'm tired, too. Let's rest for a bit."

When she rested her head against the pillow, tears licked her eyelashes. But she willed herself not to cry. Not now. Not yet.

There would be time for tears when Eli was better. When their new baby arrived. Then there would be plenty of time for tears of joy.

December 24, 6:00 P.M.

Levi backed away as the auburn-haired girl, the *Englischer*, ran to the bed and threw her arms around Melody. He stood in the doorway uneasily, at a loss for what to do. Perhaps he should leave? But that didn't seem right. He'd promised Melody he would be by her side for as long as she wanted him.

After hugging the girl tightly, Melody looked for him. "Levi?"

Like a student, he raised one hand slightly. "I'm here. By the door."

"Oh." Her expression was puzzled. "Well, um, this is Leah. She's my friend from home."

Levi nodded as Leah looked at him curiously.

Then Melody gripped her girlfriend's hand. "What in the world are you doing here?"

"I'm here to see you, of course."

"But at Christmas?"

"I didn't want you to be alone," the girl said.

Everything in Levi's being wanted to blurt that she hadn't been. Not at all. He'd been by her side. Not out of obligation, but because it had been where he'd wanted to be.

"How did you get here?" Melody asked.

Leah turned his way. "He brought me here."

Levi stared at her, stunned. "Me?"

"No," the man who suddenly appeared beside him said with a grin. "I did." Somehow managing to look at both Levi and Melody, the man said, "I'm Zack Littleton."

"Officer Zack Littleton," Leah corrected. "He's a police officer."

"Actually, I'm a highway patrolman. I work for the sheriff's department."

"We met on the way, and when way too much happened, he drove me here." Her eyes shined as she looked at the policeman standing there. "Now he's my boyfriend."

After darting a shy glance at the man standing off to the side, Melody looked back at her friend. "Truly?"

Leah flashed a smile. "I know it happened quickly, but you don't know what we've been through. I think tragedy makes your heart's decisions faster."

Levi was hoping that Leah would clarify that statement when yet another contraction weaved its way through Melody again.

Levi's heart slammed in his throat as he glanced at the clock. "They're coming faster, now. Five minutes apart."

"That one certainly did come up quick," Melody said, her voice strained. "And it is terribly strong." The skin around her mouth looked pale.

Levi yearned to reach for her. To hold her close. It was so obvious to him that she was in a terrible amount of pain.

As much pain as Rosanna had been.

But now it seemed too awkward to do so, with her friend in the room. "Do you want me to go get Mrs. Brenneman?" he offered. "You might be close to your time." He knew the lady was as scared as the rest of them, but surely she would know what to do.

Melody bit her bottom lip. "Yes? I mean, I suppose you had better . . ."

"I could help," the man—Officer Littleton—said quietly.

Melody turned to him in wonder. *"What?"*

"Before I had this job, I was an EMT. I've delivered several babies."

The stranger's words made no sense. "You were a what?" Levi asked.

"EMT stands for Emergency Medical Technician." He paused, then clarified some more. "I used to work in an ambulance."

"Zack could help you, Melody," Leah said. "I know he could."

"Even more recently as a patrolman, I've delivered babies. Not a lot." He shook his head, smiling. "But three. You wouldn't believe what happens out on the road."

Just then, another contraction rocked Melody. "Oh!" she called out before biting her lips.

Leah gripped her hand. "No matter what, I'll be by your side, Melody, but you might want to take Zack up on his offer sooner than later. He's a good man . . . and I don't know what to do."

Pain flowed through Melody's face in such a tangible way, Levi was sure he could reach out and grasp it.

Beside him, Zack tensed. Everything in the man's posture told Levi that he was used to taking responsibility in emergencies. That he was used to doing what needed to be done. It was obvious that he wanted to help, that he knew how to help Melody. But still he waited.

That hesitation assured Levi of the man's worthiness more than anything else. This man obviously knew what had happened to Melody, and was willing to let her make the decision. Even if it meant doing nothing.

"Maybe you should let him, Melody," Levi said.

"Melody? Please?" Leah whispered. "I promise, I'll be here, too."

Finally Melody looked at Zack. "If you can help me, please do," she finally bit out between pants.

The tension in the room broke free.

Immediately Zack stepped forward. "I scrubbed my hands before I walked in the room. Leah, go wash up, then ask Mrs. Brenneman for another sheet, more towels, and something to wrap the baby in." To Levi, he added, "Go get a pair of scissors. Make sure they're clean. Sharp. And bring alcohol, too. And hot water."

Just as Levi turned to go in a rush to the officer's bidding, he saw Zack quietly sit by Melody's side. "You're going to be okay," he gently murmured.

As Zack's words registered, Levi watched a change come over her. The wild, terrified look in her eyes quieted. In its place came trust. And determination.

Lifting up Melody's hand, Zack placed his fingers on her wrist, obviously taking her pulse. "Together, we're going to bring this baby in the world," Levi heard him murmur. "Just in time for Christmas Day. All right?"

Melody nodded just as Leah came running back, her arms laden with supplies.

She pushed by Levi with a brief, apologetic look . . . and then as soon as he stepped out of the room, she closed the door.

 *Chapter 24*

December 24, 7:00 P.M.

Katie didn't know if she'd ever be able to praise God enough. Eli's congestion finally seemed to be easing.

And he was now sleeping peacefully in the bed next to Jonathan, who was sound asleep, too. The picture of the two of them, finally relaxing after hours of touch and go . . . well, it was surely the most amazing of scenes. Though she, too, was exhausted, she felt just as strong a pull to check on Melody.

She couldn't believe two *Englischers* had arrived while she'd been upstairs, one Melody's friend Leah . . . and the other—wonder of wonders—a man who had worked on an ambulance.

As she walked into the kitchen, she found Levi standing practically motionless, his whole attention on Melody's closed door.

Just a few feet away, her mother and father stood together, looking like they didn't know whether to shout for joy or cry.

"I still don't understand why they're here," Katie said.

"The girl said she's a friend of Melody's," her father replied. "They've been driving through all kinds of weather to get here."

Levi stood nearby, not speaking.

Just then, the door opened a crack. A pretty auburn-haired girl with green eyes peeked out. "Levi? Do you have the towels and water yet?"

"What? Oh, no. I'll be right there." When the door closed, Levi turned to Katie's parents. "Zack will be needin' clean scissors, hot water, and towels."

Immediately, her mother poured water into a large bowl and handed Katie two hand towels. "Go take this in, I'll get the scissors."

"All right."

Levi's face looked pained as Katie walked by him and went into the room. For a moment, she ached to say something reassuring, but no words seemed appropriate. Instead, she walked to the door and let herself in.

When she walked into the bedroom, the man and Leah were counting, helping Melody breathe.

"It's almost time, I think," the man murmured. Then he turned to Katie. "Oh, good. Leah, grab that, will you?"

"I'm Leah," the girl said. "That's Zack."

"I'm glad you're here," Katie said. "I'm not really sure how you got here, but I know you were sorely needed."

When Melody moaned again, her cry high-pitched and shrill, Katie turned back out. The girl was in capable hands, her friend's, the officer's, and God's.

"How is she?" Levi asked the moment Katie returned to the kitchen.

"About as well as she can be doing, I imagine. Zack looks to be a capable person."

"I hope so."

Mrs. Brenneman patted his shoulder. "It's a difficult thing, being the one to wait. But it's how it's done."

Katie fixed a mug of hot tea for herself, and one for him as well. When she set it in front of him, Levi stared at it glumly.

"Take a sip. You'll be glad for it."

"*Danke.*"

"I think everything is going to be all right," Katie murmured with more assurance than she'd ever felt before in her life. "Don't you feel him with us tonight?"

"Him?"

"Our Lord? Levi, think about it. Here we are all, together. A houseful of scattered individuals. It makes no sense that so much should have happened. So much during tonight, of all nights."

Her mom nodded, her cheeks pink. "I must say, this is a Christmas like I've never experienced. I had planned for my family to sit and relax. Spend time reading. Doing puzzles. Going for walks. Baking. But here, we've all been entangled in your story. And Melody's! Now, I promise I wouldn't have wanted it any other way."

Levi slowly relaxed beside her. "If the Lord brought me here, I hope he's still watching over us."

Down the hall, Melody let out a cry. Beside her, Katie watched Levi grip the kitchen counter hard. Unable to say anything more, she simply held out her hand to him. Then bowed her head and prayed. His hand covering hers, he did the same.

She prayed silently, as was their way. But she prayed with all her heart. She thanked the Lord for being with her and Eli. Thanked him that he guided her through her selfishness, and through each person's own worries and concerns.

She asked him to be with Melody. And with Zack. And with Leah, too.

And because the sense of peace felt so wonderful— because she felt so close to God, as though he was holding her other hand—she silently said it all again.

Down the hall, Melody cried out again. And then, miracles of miracles, a far different cry was heard.

Tears were in her eyes when Katie opened them again.

Across the kitchen, her mother clasped her hands together and beamed. "Praise God. A child is born."

Beside her, Levi wiped his cheeks with a fist. "Indeed," he murmured. Then he finally smiled, too.

Chapter 25

December 25, 6:00 A.M.

"That had to have been the most incredible night of my life," Leah gushed to Melody the next morning.

After Melody had given birth to the most perfect little girl in the world, Leah and Mrs. Brenneman had helped her get settled, then she and her baby had fallen into an exhausted slumber. Now, just as dawn was breaking on Christmas Day, she was holding Faith in bed. Leah had just come in to help Melody wash and get dressed.

Now Melody was more than happy to let Leah continue to chatter like a magpie about the wondrous events in her life.

"I mean, Melody, who would have ever thought I could have fallen in love on the way to see you?"

"Not I." Though she'd only heard snippets about the romance, Melody had to agree that it did indeed seem incredible. "Are you sure it's love, though?"

"Yes." A new awareness shone in Leah's eyes. "I've been infatuated before. I've liked other men a lot. Sometimes I've wondered if the relationship I was in was going to turn into love. But never before have I felt anything like this. What I feel for Zack is so strong. So right. It must have been meant to be."

"I imagine so."

"Gosh, are you laughing at me?" Leah grinned. "Even if you are, I don't care. I'm just so happy."

"I'm not laughing." In her arms, tiny Faith made a little fist, then relaxed her hand and continued to sleep. Both Mrs. Brenneman and Katie had warned her that newborns slept almost constantly their first twenty-four hours. Melody was glad they'd told her, otherwise she was sure she would be very nervous.

Looking at Leah, she shook her head in wonder. "I just can't believe you are here. When you appeared in the doorway, I promise, at first I thought you were a dream."

"I didn't want you to be alone." Turning serious, Leah murmured, "This whole time, I've been so worried about you, Melody. I haven't understood why any of this happened."

"I don't think we had to understand, at least not right now. Perhaps one day we will?"

"Maybe you're right. Anyway, I can't tell you how nice the Brenneman family has been to me. When we left you last night, Mr. Brenneman had two rooms ready for Zack and me."

"They are truly the nicest people. They've made me feel so welcome and almost like I was a part of their family," said Melody. "It's been a wonderful gift. Now, how long do you intend to stay?"

"As long as you'd like me to."

"What about Zack?"

"I think he took off until December twenty-seventh."

"My bus reservation is on the morning of the twenty-seventh."

"Melody, there's no way I'm going to let you and Faith travel home on a bus! You can return with Zack and me."

"Are you sure? I don't want to be any trouble."

Leah grinned. "Too late. If you thought my being here was like a dream, traveling here was a nightmare."

Melody chuckled, because she knew Leah didn't mean anything bad. "Then I can only hope that the return trip will be far better. But you had better ask Zack first, Leah. Don't you think?"

"I'll ask him, but I can't imagine why he'd say no."

"Last night, I was so thankful he was here."

"He's an amazing man. Nothing seems to faze him, Melody."

As Melody thought again of how his take-charge attitude had steadied her fears and brought a new sense of calm to the room, she knew she'd always be grateful.

After a brief knock, Katie Brenneman peeked inside. "Good morning! Merry Christmas!"

"Good morning to you," Melody said.

"Can I come in?"

"Please do! And please meet Faith."

"Ah. Yes, Faith is a wonderful-*gut* name for your *boppli*." Katie leaned forward and admired her with a soft smile. "She's beautiful. And so tiny."

"Zack thought she was six pounds."

"My Eli was almost eight when he was born. No wonder she looks so small." Turning to Leah, Katie murmured, "We're having breakfast now. Your Zack has been sitting with us, but I have to say he is looking a little lost out there, sitting among the Amish."

Leah stood up abruptly, then bit her lip as she glanced Melody's way. "I'm sorry. Do you mind—"

"I'd mind if you let Zack sit in there all by himself! Go now."

"We'll be back after we eat. I know he'd love to see you and Faith again, first thing."

"I'll see you after breakfast."

Katie grinned as she took the chair Leah vacated in a flash. She and Melody watched her practically run out the door, and she said, "Your friend is smitten."

"It sure seems that way." As she looked at Katie, she noticed dark smudges under her eyes. "Are you all right? How is your boy? I remember he was sick?"

"He's better, *danke*. He's still sick, but his fever is down, and the steam steeped with peppermint seems to have helped a great deal."

"I'm glad."

"May I bring you some tea or coffee?"

"I'd love some coffee."

Katie stood up. "I'll bring it right out to you. My *mamm*

made homemade cinnamon rolls this morning, too. Would you care for one of those?"

"Your mother is a wonder, making cinnamon rolls so early. She must not have ever gone to sleep!"

"She is a wonder, but these rolls are easier than most. They use a box of yellow cake mix."

"I would love to have one, although I feel bad, with you having to wait on me."

"Don't feel bad at all. I'm glad to help you, Melody." She stepped away, then turned back to her. "Listen, I don't want to forget to say this. I . . . I am glad you are here. I know I wasn't at first, and I know I've already apologized, but I don't think it will ever be too much to tell you I'm sorry again."

"There's no need."

"I think there is. I'm ashamed. I just wanted you to know that your visit has been a joyous event for our family. I, for one, will always be grateful that you came here." She pursed her lips. "And, I just want you to know . . . I think you're very brave."

Melody was too choked up to immediately reply. "Your words mean a great deal," she whispered. *"Danke."*

Moments after Katie left to get her some breakfast, Melody leaned back on the cushions of the bed. Once again, all her attention turned to her precious Faith. "What a miracle this Christmas has been," she murmured. "It's a miracle that everything has turned out so well."

The well-known verse from 1 Corinthians floated through her mind. People often talked about that verse for romantic love, but she remembered someone telling her once that Paul's talk of love hadn't really been meant for romance. He was talking about love of faith. Love of each other. Love that was strong and patient and kind.

And that's how she felt when she looked at her baby. Suddenly, all the ugliness that had filled her life didn't seem to matter anymore. Suddenly, all that really mattered was here in her arms.

"I brought you coffee," Levi said from the doorway.

"Levi!" She didn't even try to contain her smile for him.

"May I come in?"

"Of course. I'm so glad to see you. Would . . . would you care to meet my daughter?"

Warily he stepped forward, gingerly handling the coffee mug like he was afraid he'd spill it. She noticed he hardly looked at her until he put the coffee cup down. Only then did he straighten and look her way.

His expression turned awed. "Oh, but she's beautiful, Melody."

"I think so, too."

He looked so wistful, so overcome, she motioned him closer. "Would you like to hold her?"

"No, I couldn't." But he did step closer.

"Why not?" Gently, she held her arms out to him. "Hold her, Levi. After all, she's in your debt."

Almost as if he was in a trance, he took Faith from her, taking special care to hold the baby's head and neck securely. Melody had to smile—Faith looked even smaller in his big hands. She hadn't thought such a thing was possible.

Slowly, he sat down, hardly lifting his eyes from Faith's peaceful face. Still her little girl slept on.

Finally, he met her gaze. "Why would you say she was in my debt?"

"It was a poor joke, I suppose. But how could I not feel beholden to you? You stayed with me, because I asked. You comforted me because I needed you—even though being in this room had to be a terribly difficult thing." Though she knew she was stumbling over her words, Melody kept trying to make Levi see things from her point of view. "Levi, quite honestly, I don't know how I would have gotten through yesterday if you hadn't been by my side."

"But I didn't do anything. It was Zack and Leah who helped you deliver."

"Only at the very end." Reaching out, she pressed her palm on his arm. "Levi, I know you would have helped me if they wouldn't have come."

"I would have. But I'm glad I didn't have to."

As she watched the man she'd come to trust so much hold her baby, Melody felt a contentment she hadn't known would be possible to feel.

With a start, she realized she was feeling much of the same emotions toward him that she did with Faith. Longing to be with him as much as possible.

Sometime over the course of her visit, and their time together, she'd fallen in love. She, who'd assumed she'd never trust a man again.

Though Levi's coffee was delicious, the previous day's exertions still left her exhausted. She tried hard to resist, but her eyelids grew heavy. "Levi, would you mind watching over Faith for me? Just for a little while?" A yawn escaped her. "Suddenly, I'm so tired . . ."

And suddenly, she felt so warm and content. She let herself lower her defenses.

She let herself sleep.

Levi blinked as he realized what had happened. Melody had fallen asleep . . . and had entrusted him with Faith.

In his arms, the tiny baby slept as well. She was so light in his arms, he knew he could have held her all day. And her expression was so sweet, it tore the last of his layers of grief away. Now he could only find hope in his heart. Hope and love for Faith . . . and a growing love for Melody, too.

When Faith shifted her arm, Levi warily looked at the bed. Melody had made a little area right next to her for the babe.

Perhaps the right thing to do would be to set Faith there and give Melody her privacy?

Yes. That was the right thing to do, for sure. As gently as he could, he set Faith next to Melody and hovered, just to make sure she didn't cry.

But instead of fretting, the babe shifted, then continued her slumber. Looking like an angel from heaven.

In front of him was a sight he'd always imagined seeing. Of course, the woman wasn't his wife. And the baby wasn't the girl who'd died with Rosanna. But for just a few moments, he could imagine that this was his family.

That these girls were his heart.

And so he sat down again. Just in case he was needed.

As Melody slumbered, he took the opportunity to gaze at her. To look upon every feature in a way he would have never allowed himself to do if she was awake. Her hair was slick, silky to the touch.

His fingers twitched as he remembered brushing it away from her face.

Her cheeks held the faint bloom of a blush. He remembered they'd burned bright red in embarrassment when he dared to ask her about her past. And had sweetly pinked when she caught him staring at her for too long.

Her lips, so perfectly formed, gently moved with each breath. He remembered when she'd first smiled at him . . . and at how dazzled he'd felt. He imagined kissing her, of holding her close in his arms.

He couldn't deny the truth any longer. He was enchanted by Melody.

And by tiny Faith, of course. A yearning for a child of his own. Forcing himself to look at the baby, he knew there was no greater gift than a newborn baby. How could he ever have asked Melody if she'd planned to keep Faith?

How could anyone look at Faith and only see ugliness? Surely not him.

Burgeoning inside of him was the warm, sweet feeling of happiness. Of protection.

Of hope.

For the first time in ages, he actually wanted to make plans. He ached to ask Melody when he could come visit. Ached to ask if he could write to her.

And . . . he wanted other things, too. Marriage. A life beside her.

But even the idea of asking for her hand gave him pause. How would she react to such demands? Would she yearn to forget him? To try and put all the experiences they had shared out of her mind?

Steeling himself, he knew he had to try. He wanted to see her again as soon as possible. Even waiting two weeks sounded like too much.

For better or worse . . . she had become his heart.

A faint knock startled him. Turning, he watched the door open as Leah peeked in. "Hi. Am I interrupting anything?"

"*Nee*. Melody is sleeping."

"And you're just watching them sleep?"

"I, uh, I just lost track of time, I suppose," he murmured. Since Leah still stood there, looking at him curiously, he got to his feet. "I should probably go."

"Don't worry. I'll keep watch over Faith."

"Yes. Yes, that's very good. I'll um, just leave you now." With effort, he walked out the door. Already at a loss.

Already wishing he'd had a reason to stay.

Chapter 26

December 25, 10:00 A.M.

"When can we open presents, Katie?" Mary asked. "We've been so patient."

Katie shared a knowing look with her mother. Though Santa Claus didn't pay them a visit, of course, the girls each had three or four packages sitting on a windowsill, their fancy green and red wrappings making the room look bright and merry.

Katie had also brought from her room a few other special gifts . . . one for her mother, and two others, one for Winnie and one for Anna. A part of her was as eager as a child to share her offerings.

But was it appropriate to exchange gifts now, with guests nearby? She looked to her parents for guidance.

As if he could read her mind, her father nodded slowly. "I think opening a few gifts right now would be a fine idea. Though much has been happening around here, it is still Christmas Day. We can't lose sight of that."

"I agree," her mother said. "Once again, we have much to be thankful for. The snow and ice only serve to highlight that."

Hannah clapped her hands as she scampered out of the room. "I'll go find everyone and bring them in here."

Katie chuckled as she followed her parents to the hearth room. Moments later, Jonathan came in with a load of wood, Zack, Henry, and Sam behind him.

"Daed!" Mary called out. "It's time to open my presents."

"Who says?"

"Daadi—Grandpa, that's who."

Jonathan's face turned serious. "Then I guess I had best do as he says, yes?" After sharing a smile with Katie, he said, "Let me wash my hands and get more coffee. The weather outside near froze me through."

When Sam and Henry mentioned they would do the same, Katie stood up and walked to Zack. "I hope you don't mind that we have a bit of family time now? Of course, if you'd like, you'd be most welcome to join us."

Zack waved off her remarks with a lopsided grin. "This is a time just for family, I think. I'd be sad if you put off opening presents because we're here. I just wanted to tell you that I was going to help myself to coffee and then go find Leah."

"She's in with Melody and Levi," Anna supplied.

"I'll go there, then."

As Winnie entered the room, Katie's mother spoke to Zack. "Please help yourself to coffee and some warm cinnamon rolls, too. We'll have a real breakfast soon, with eggs and potatoes and sausages."

"No worries," Zack said over his shoulder as he left. "Those rolls smell so good, I'm sure they'll suit me fine."

Soon, it was just their wonderful extended family again. Katie held Eli while Jonathan chatted with Mary and Hannah. Nearby Anna and Henry sat together, looking for all the world like a pair of newlyweds. Every so often, Anna would sneak a glance Henry's way and he would smile back. Or pat her shoulder.

On the other side of the room sat Winnie and Sam. Their marriage never failed to make Katie smile. While Anna and Henry's relationship might be classified as more tender and circumspect, Winnie and Sam's marriage seemed to be filled with talk and teasing. Samuel's brilliant mind had sparked a curiosity in Winnie that Katie hadn't ever realized was under the surface. Now she seemed most interested in just about everything around her, and that curiosity seemed to suit Samuel just fine.

As at that very moment—sitting there across from Katie, the pair was teasing each other about Winnie's proposed garden, and what to plant first. She noticed that Sam was holding Winnie's hand in between the both of his while they traded barbs.

Finally, near the fireplace, sat her parents. It was no exaggeration to say they were the heart and soul of her family. Though they'd been up as late as everyone else, their expressions were bright as they watched Mary and Hannah chat up a storm and wiggle with anticipation.

Once everyone was settled, it was time to exchange gifts. Standing up, her father walked to the corner behind the fireplace and pulled out a beautiful walking stick. The top was hand carved into an octagon shape. Just like the other canes and sticks he carved, at first glance it looked deceptively simple, then further inspection revealed true craftsmanship.

He cleared his throat. "Jonathan, I made this for you."

Her husband looked at the cane with a bit of awe. "*Danke*. It's a beautiful piece of work."

Henry—being Henry—seemed to not be able to refrain from teasing. "Daed, are you starting to worry about Jonathan gettin' around all right? He *is* getting older . . ."

"I only worry about him when my grandson is up in the middle of the night fussing. And fussing."

Jonathan chuckled, too. "On nights like that, I feel like I am in dire need of a cane!"

Hannah jumped up. "Do we need to wait much longer to open *our* presents?"

"Not another minute," Katie said. "Go open them now."

As she'd expected, the girls looked pleased with their new nightgowns and overjoyed to have robes from a department store . . . the fabric was incredibly soft, just like a newborn lamb's coat.

But Katie found her eyes widening with the girls when they opened the next two presents . . . baby dolls. Not 'Amish' handmade ones, either. These were real looking, with eyes and soft smiles. They looked so dear. "Mamm, you spoil them."

"Not so much." With a gentle smile at the girls, she said, "I thought you might enjoy having your own babies for a bit."

"Just like Eli!"

"Except these won't fuss as much or as loudly," Mary added.

With her heart swelling with love and pride, Katie opened up the lid to her sewing basket and pulled out the star quilt she'd labored over for so many nights. "Mary, this is for you. A Christmas quilt."

Mary's eyes widened as she examined the colorful, bright star. "Oh, Katie! How did you make it without me seeing?"

Jonathan grunted. "In the middle of the night."

Mary ran a hand over the quilt again, making Katie realize that all her hard work was worth every minute. "I love it. It's *wunderbaar*!"

Anna came over and knelt next to Mary. "This is truly beautiful work, Katie. Oh, Mary, what a treasure!"

Then, of course, it was time for the girls to hand their grandmother the set of placemats they'd worked so hard to piece together and stitch carefully.

Winnie and Samuel gave each other packets of seeds.

Anna gave Henry a shirt. "I made it myself," she declared proudly. "And this one, I actually think you'll be able to wear!"

Henry held it up in front of him. "Ah. Yes, this time the arms are the same length," he said. "*Danke*, my *liewe*."

As Katie watched everyone exchange their simple gifts to each other, her whole being filled with joy. This was what she'd been looking forward to when they'd all planned to spend a week together at the inn. Time together.

"*Mamm*," Mary ventured, "did you get Daed anything?"

They'd already agreed not to exchange gifts. With Eli's birth, and the chance for all to be here at the inn, Katie knew there wouldn't be a single other thing in the world that she needed.

But it was Jonathan who answered. "A little over a year ago, when Katie agreed to marry me, she gave me her heart and reminded me about togetherness again. She's given me joy and trust."

She looked at her husband with happiness. Oh, but he was such a good man. A kind one. "I feel the same way," she said.

Then, to her surprise, he stood up, left the room, and returned with a cloak. A beautifully made cloak in black, with a soft lining, too. "But I did think you could use a new cloak, Katie. This one should keep you warm all winter long. You and the babe," he whispered.

She knew the coat symbolized so many things. It would cover her body and keep her warm. It symbolized the shelter she'd so often yearned for years ago.

And every time she would put it over her shoulders, she knew she'd remember the joy of this day. "I love it," she said simply. Then, she reached out to him and nodded.

Positively beaming with pride, he reached for her hand and looked around the room again. "Just last night, Katie told me she had yet another present for me . . . a new baby is on the way."

The room erupted in cheers as Anna and Winnie rushed forward, followed by Katie's mother and father.

"Why didn't you tell us?" Winnie exclaimed.

"I don't know. At first, I didn't want to believe it was true. Then I wanted to first tell Jonathan . . ." She sighed as a lump formed in her throat. "And, truthfully, I was worried. I wasn't too happy about having another child so soon."

"And now?" Winnie searched her gaze. Katie instinctively knew that her sister-in-law would do anything she possibly could to make things easier.

"Now I realize I've been silly. I should have given up my burdens to the Lord, to Jonathan, and to all of you. With your help, nothing is too great a burden."

Her mother wiped her eyes. "I have to say, this has been a wonderful-*gut* Christmas already. Melody's baby was born, and now your news, too!"

After another round of hugs, Henry wrapped an arm around Anna. "Daed? Will you now make our Christmas complete?"

"Of course. But, I wonder if perhaps we should ask our guests if they'd care to join us?"

Henry got to his feet. "I'll go ask."

Twenty minutes later, the room was even more crowded. Zack and Leah had come in, their jeans and sweatshirts looking cozy and warm. Next to Leah sat Melody in a thick flannel nightgown and Katie's fleece robe. Holding little Faith was Levi, his expression one of wonder . . . and for the first time . . . hope.

"Yes, this feels like the right time now," her father murmured. "I'll get our good Book."

As he had for as long as she could remember, her father stood up, walked across the room, and picked up his Bible. Though Henry had been sitting right next to it, and it would have been an easy thing for him to reach over and snatch it from the desktop, Katie knew Henry would not have grasped the Book without his father's asking any more than she ever would have. It wasn't how they did things.

It wasn't their family's way.

Every Christmas Day, in the evening, after everyone had eaten a wonderful-*gut* dinner with all their favorites, and after the children had opened a present or two, their father would take down the Bible and read from the book of Luke.

But now it felt like the time was right there, on this special morning. Sitting curled up next to their father, Mary and Hannah watched their adopted grandfather carefully slip on his reading glasses and turn back the pages.

And though Katie knew what he was about to say— though she could practically have recited the text on her own—she found herself leaning forward in anticipation of the story. Just like the girls did.

Just as she did so long ago.

Her *daed* cleared his throat. "And so it was," he began. "In those days a decree went out from the Emperor Augustus that all the world should be registered."

As he continued to read the Bible story, a wondrous

sense of peace settled over her. This was what Christmas was all about—Jesus's birth. This is what she should have been focusing on. Not her own selfish wishes. Not her troubles.

She should have been focusing on the joy of her savior's birth, and the miracle of his life.

Later, her father said the words she knew so well. "In that region there were shepherds living in the fields, keeping watch over their flock by night. Then an angel of the Lord stood before them, and the glory of the Lord shone around them, and they were terrified. But the angel said to them, 'Do not be afraid.'"

As he continued, Katie looked toward Henry, who smiled as well. Then she turned to her husband, whom she loved so very dearly. Whom she'd loved for what felt like all her life.

He looked right back. Love and patience filled his eyes. And happiness.

She'd been so silly. He was happy about a new baby to love, not upset at the burden! At that moment, she knew that he would support her no matter what, and would willingly change his life to better accommodate hers.

"Later," she mouthed. Yes, later, they would sit alone and make plans again. Together, they would figure out how to manage everything.

They would have plenty of time for that. And time to give thanks, too.

Chapter 27

December 26, 9:00 A.M.

Levi stood in the front entryway next to Melody as the Brennemans bustled about. For the last hour, everyone had been doing their best to help get all of Melody's belongings together. Now Zack and Leah were outside, preparing Zack's truck to hold an additional two passengers.

He'd been unwilling to leave her side for a minute.

So as everyone else rushed around, Levi watched over Melody and tiny Faith . . . and tried not to look too despondent.

As quickly as Christmas had come upon them, it was now over. As was Melody's visit to the Brenneman Bed and Breakfast.

And though Melody had originally planned to stay longer, Levi knew it made perfect sense for her to leave with her girlfriend and the highway patrolman. If Melody stayed another day, she would be forced to return on the bus alone.

That, of course, would not be good. This way, Melody would be watched over by two caring people. And, of course, it would be far safer for tiny Faith to travel in Zack's truck than in the crowded bus.

Yes, it made perfect sense. It was right for Melody to leave with Zack and Leah this morning.

Of course.

But Levi was still anticipating her loss like a physical thing. He'd hoped for more time with her. To give Melody more opportunities to get to know him. And to want to see him again.

As Melody shifted Faith in her arms, he turned to her. "Are you sure you don't want to sit down? I could pull over a chair from the parlor."

"I'm certain. It feels *gut* to stand up for a bit. And I'll be sitting for hours soon enough. It's a mighty long drive back to Kentucky."

Yes, it was very far. So terribly far from his own home.

"Yes. I imagine it is." It took Levi everything he had to keep his expression neutral and his voice even. "Are you sure you don't need to stay another day or two? Perhaps Leah could be persuaded to stay longer if you needed that time. Then you could both travel on the bus."

Genuine regret filled her gaze. "I can't ask that of her.

And once more, I don't think I should. Zack needs to get back. So does Leah. If I leave with them, they can take me."

Yes, it did make perfect sense. But already his heart felt close to breaking. They hadn't had enough time together.

"It might be a mistake to travel, but, Levi, I'm beginning to realize this whole trip was probably a mistake."

Her words hit him like a blow to his stomach. "You truly wish you had never come here?"

She winced. "Oh, I didn't mean that how it sounded. I'm glad I was here to meet you. Mighty glad. But you have to admit, yesterday was a scary time. Never would I have guessed that I was going to give birth in the middle of a snowstorm on Christmas Eve."

To say it had been a shock was putting it mildly. But it had been a day of miracles, too. With Faith's birth, he'd been able to bury some of the guilt he'd been carrying around about Rosanna's death.

It was now obvious that there was nothing else he could have done. For reasons known only to the Lord, he'd decided to take Rosanna to his heart early.

And now, he'd gifted Melody with a wide band of people who cared about her and prayed with her. And Levi. He felt a strong pull. More than ever, Levi was certain a future with Melody was God's will. It was his greatest desire as well.

It took everything he had not to reach out and touch her. Not to smooth away the stray lock of hair that had fallen on her forehead. But it wasn't his place. Not yet, anyway.

Levi noticed the hustle and bustle around them had finally slowed. "Perhaps everyone is just about ready now."

She bit her lip. "Yes. It does seem that way. And that's probably a good thing, right?"

"Since it's a long journey."

"Yes. It's a day's journey under the best of conditions . . ."

"And it's certainly not that now," he finished for her.

"No, it's not." Melody drew a ragged breath, obviously trying not to cry. "I imagine we'll be all right, though. Zack's truck has heat, and the Brennemans have packed me a little tote full of things for Faith." Turning her head, she gazed at her baby again. "It's lucky that Katie was here, and that she and her mother had diapers and clothes for a newborn."

"It was lucky, indeed."

With effort, Levi forced himself to act detached. It wouldn't do for him to act too forward. It would be wrong of him to ask her to stay.

Yes. What she was doing made perfect sense. Plus, she needed to return home. Her parents needed to know about Faith's birth. They were no doubt worried about her.

Clearly, the only reason for her to stay would be his selfishness. Pure and simple, he wanted another day with her.

He wanted more for his memories. And, of course, he wanted more time to perhaps encourage her to think of him in her life. To imagine him being a part of her life, as she was in his. Levi knew Melody was now such an integral part of his being, she would never leave. Her image could never be erased.

Whatever plans God had for him, no matter what, no

matter what happened in the future, Levi knew without a doubt that his heart belonged to a petite woman from Kentucky.

Leah blew in. "I think we're all set. Zack already has your suitcase. Henry carried it out the back door and handed it to him."

"So all we have left is my bag here."

Leah picked up the shopping bag and her tote. "Done. Now, the only thing left to do is gather up you and Faith."

With another long look at Levi, Melody rearranged Faith in her arms again. Fussing with the blanket, making sure the babe was as toasty as she could be for the short walk to Zack's truck. "I suppose I'm all set, now."

Levi felt like his mouth was full of cotton. No words were able to escape. As Leah led the way, Melody and Faith followed, and he trailed behind. At a loss.

The Brenneman family was waiting for them.

Tears filled Mrs. Brenneman's eyes as she approached first. "Oh, Melody. I can't believe we're telling you good-bye already. What a blessing it was for you to come here."

"You can still say that after everything?"

"Most definitely." She wrapped Melody in a warm hug. "Don't be a stranger, now. And please write. And please remember that you are welcome anytime. Anytime! As our guest."

"May God be with you, Melody," Mr. Brenneman said.

Next Katie approached, her eyes filled with tears as well. "Your being here has been so special. It's changed my life. You've changed my life, Melody."

She felt the same way. For some reason, Melody knew

that her visit at the Brennemans' inn had been meant to be. And that she was a better person for the experience.

But all that felt like too much. "I will miss you."

"We want to see you soon."

"I will try," she promised. In truth, nothing could make her happier than another visit to the inn.

Next came the rest of the family. Melody noticed that Levi took care to stand to one side as one by one each approached, hugged her close, and took one last adoring look at Faith.

Then the only person left to say goodbye to was Levi. Turning to Leah, who'd been hovering nearby, she asked, "Could you take Faith for a moment?"

"Sure. I'll go to the truck." Giving Melody a meaningful look, she murmured, "Take your time."

Her heart beating fast, Melody walked to where Levi stood. Off to the side. "I guess this is goodbye."

"I . . . I will miss you."

"I will miss you, too." Oh, there was so much she wanted to say, but not here, in front of everyone.

Gently, he reached out and placed a finger under her chin. Pressed slightly until she was looking into his eyes. "Don't forget that I'll write you."

"I promise I will write you back."

He nodded. Then, to her surprise, he said nothing more, just enfolded her in his arms. Not caring what anyone thought, she rested her head on his shoulder and hugged him back.

Oh, how she wished she could take all his goodness, all his warmth home with her!

His arms tightened around her. She felt the briefest of kisses on her head. And then he stepped away. "They're waiting," he said, his voice thick with emotion. "It's time."

"Yes. I suppose it is. Goodbye, Levi. Goodbye . . . and thank you."

He smiled gently, then turned away.

The only thing to do was walk to the truck. Each step away from him felt like a mile.

 # Chapter 28

December 28, noon

"You went away for Christmas, didn't you?" Kevin asked around a bite of roast beef sandwich.

Levi swallowed his own bite of ham as he nodded.

Yesterday, when he'd traveled all day to get home, he'd been too occupied with his own thoughts. Too often he'd find himself looking out the window and being reminded of Melody. The golden sunrise reminded him of her eyes. The shy tilt of a woman's chin at a rest stop made him think of her as well. He had been looking forward to going back to work just so he wouldn't be remembering so much.

But with one question from his boss, he was transported back again to the inn.

"Where did you go?"

"Cincinnati."

Kevin looked at him in surprise. "That's quite a ways. What was there?"

"An inn. I had heard about a special bed-and-breakfast, the Brenneman Bed and Breakfast. It's family owned." Still struggling with how to make his words sound nonchalant, he shrugged. "I thought it would be a good place for me to be."

"Ah. Did you enjoy yourself?"

Had he? It had been an eventful visit, that was for sure. But enjoyable? Was falling in love unexpectedly an enjoyable thing? "I did enjoy myself."

"I bet it did you good to get away," Kevin murmured. "Are Christmases still as painful as ever?"

It was sometimes a surprise to realize everything he'd taken such care to hide hadn't been hidden at all. "I had thought it would be a painful time, but it was an easier thing."

"Then you made the right choice, going away."

"Perhaps." Now, instead of only thinking about Rosanna's death on Christmas Eve, he found himself reliving the miracle of Faith's birth. "As a matter of fact, I think the pain has lessened quite a bit."

"What did you do with your time?" Ivan asked from across the table. "I think I'd be bored silly, sitting by myself at a bed-and-breakfast."

"I was planning to be bored. Actually looking forward to it, but I wasn't that way at all. For one thing, we went hunting." And, of course, he'd fallen in love.

Kevin raised his eyebrows. "I didn't know you hunted."

"I don't. But the men invited me along, and I enjoyed myself. They got a six-point buck."

"You got lucky."

"We did. Other things were exciting as well," he allowed. "A storm came and turned the area pitch black, right on Christmas Eve. And while we were stranded in the dark, another guest gave birth to a baby." He was proud of himself for sounding so matter-of-fact. So easy. His palms still shook when he recalled how afraid he'd been.

Kevin and the other men in the room who'd recently joined them looked shocked. "Well, there's a story right there," Ivan quipped. "A baby born on Christmas in an inn—just like in the Bible."

"It was quite an event." It was on the tip of his tongue to try and describe just how remarkable a time it had been . . . but of course, there was no way he could reveal his story without giving Melody's private business away.

So he ate his sandwich, listened to the other men talk of lumber prices and cranky wives, eating too much ham and other travels. And as the other men talked, Levi let his mind drift again to Melody and the last look she gave him before slipping into Zack's truck and taking off.

Last night he'd written her. The note had been short and to the point. He asked after her trip and inquired about her health. Of course he also wished for Faith's continued health as well.

There was so much he'd ached to say, to ask . . . but had been afraid. He wondered how her parents were treating her. He wondered if she was happier, or if she still held the thick cord of grief around herself. Cutting off so much to the outside world.

Later that afternoon, he went to the store and picked up some freshly roasted chicken from the Yoder's market. While inside, he saw his neighbors.

"We heard you were back, Levi. We're glad of it."

"Thank you. I'm glad, too."

They exchanged pleasantries, talking about much of the same things that he'd discussed with the men at work. And then he went home and carefully prepared a dish and ate in the silence.

After the rest of his chores, the rest of the night dragged on. Giving him all the incentive he needed to pick up a pencil again and write. Now, at least, he could tell her about his workday. Perhaps that would interest her some?

It had to be better than to hear him pine for her again. Because that's all he seemed to be able to do.

But he had to write. He had to keep that connection. In truth, he couldn't bear the thought of having Melody out of his life.

As if he had a choice.

December 30, 2:00 P.M.

"A letter's come for you, Melody," her mother practically sang as she flew though the front door. "It's another one from Berlin." After setting the envelope on the table beside Melody's rocking chair, she looked at Melody expectantly.

"*Danke, Mamm.*"

"Well, aren't you going to open it?"

"I will in a little while." No way did she want to read the letter in front of her mother. It was too personal. Too special.

"Oh."

Though Faith was sleeping contentedly beside her and didn't need her attention, Melody kept her eyes on the baby. Her feelings about Levi were too raw to even hide. She had a hunch that one look would reveal far too much to her mother.

But of course she didn't take the hint. "What is this Levi like? Why is he writing you so often?"

Well, she supposed some things couldn't be put off forever. After taking a sip of the hot peppermint tea for fortification, she said, "He's a good man. Quiet, I suppose. We became friends of a sort at the inn."

"I suppose that's only natural. After all, there weren't many people there, right? Mainly family?"

"That's right. There was only the Brenneman family, me, and Levi."

"And so because you spent so much time together, you two became close?"

Thinking back to their relationship, back to their walk, their time putting together the puzzle or sitting at the table with the family, Melody knew there was no easy way to describe their connection. "We did."

"Exactly how close?"

Melody looked at her mom. Everything about her was full of hope, full of optimistic interest. With some surprise, she realized her mother was happy that Melody had reached out to anyone.

That realization helped Melody lower her guard a tiny bit. "As close as two people with little in common can get, I suppose." Melody felt slightly guilty about smoothing over their many common traits, but she felt a little diffident about them, too. After all, they'd only spent six days together.

After all, could a relationship ever be based on a history of regrets?

"Perhaps he will come out this way and visit?"

"Perhaps. He, uh, said he would."

"Would you care for that?"

"Of course. It is always nice to have company." Melody felt her mother's frustration like a tangible thing, but she didn't care. This letter beside her was only the second one he'd sent, and the first hadn't been all that personal.

But it still hadn't stopped her heart from beating a little bit faster when she scanned his note. It still hadn't prevented a little seedling of hope to spring forth, allowing her to imagine another life than the one she was living.

Another life that was better. Not that things were so terrible now, of course. If anything, a new sense of peace had bloomed in her family, in a way that Melody hadn't imagined would be possible.

From the moment she'd gotten home, her parents had done nothing but treat Faith with love and awe. Her father had taken to being the first person to pick up her daughter the moment she made a peep.

And her sister May, well, May had been especially

kind. Gone were the stilted conversations where her sister seemed to want to pretend that Melody had gotten pregnant by herself. Gone were the endless questions about her future.

Now things were settled, calm. Perhaps it was time to even contemplate her future.

"Mother, have I thanked you for everything?"

"Thanked me?" She leaned forward, the muscles in her neck cording, revealing her tension. "For what?"

"You know."

She shook her head. The confusion on her face couldn't be masked. With a start, Melody realized that her mother really didn't know what she'd done. "You put your personal beliefs aside and got me help. Let me go to the counselor. And now, you and Daed are treating Faith with so much love . . ." Her voice drifted off.

They had done so much! How was it possible to sum it up as a mere list?

With a crack of her knees, her mother knelt in front of her and clasped her hands. "Child, you have everything all wrong. Your father and I never 'let' you go to the hospital or 'let' you get counseling in spite of our wishes, it was what we wanted. We yearned for you to heal. To feel better."

"But you always seemed so upset."

"We've been upset because of your circumstances, Melody, we didn't push our feelings aside. We did just the opposite! We put everything we had toward you. I'm sorry if it didn't seem that way."

Before Melody could even figure out how to respond, there was a knock at the front door. "We have a visitor."

"I tell you, life never seems to slow down, now, does it?" With a sigh, her mother climbed to her feet. "I'll get it."

Two minutes later, Leah raced in, bringing with her the fresh scent of winter and cold. And a truly beautiful smile. Melody stood up and hugged her. "This is a surprise."

"It shouldn't be. You should have known I wouldn't be able to stay away. How's our girl?"

"She is fine. Sleepy." Her whole being seemed to swell with a love and pride she'd only imagined.

Leah knelt down in front of the bassinet. Gently, she pulled back Faith's pink fleece blanket. "Oh, Melody," she breathed. "She is so absolutely precious."

"I think so."

"And she already looks bigger!"

"I hope she is. My sister and I took her to the doctor yesterday for a checkup. The nurse said she was as healthy and precious a babe that she'd ever seen."

"I'll tell Zack. He'll be so excited."

"So . . . you've been talking to him?"

"Pretty much nonstop. Several times a day he's either calling me or I'm calling him. Or we're texting each other on our cell phones."

"Oh, my." An unfamiliar pang of jealousy for English toys hit her hard. What she would give to be able to hear Levi's voice. To have a conversation with him . . . to have a chance to see if what they'd shared at the inn was more than the simple product of two people spending time together.

Eyes glowing, Leah added, "He's coming out here tomorrow to meet my mom."

"That sounds mighty serious." She'd been anxious to ask Leah all about her new relationship with the handsome policeman, but they'd never had time to talk. In the car on the way home, Leah had been sitting up front by Zack's side. She had been in the backseat of the cab, dozing off and on with Faith.

Then, of course, had been the excitement and commotion of her arrival home, with a baby.

Slowly, Leah nodded. "We really are. Actually, I think he's the one."

"Oh, my! What does your *mamm* think?"

"What do you think?" she asked dryly. "She thinks I've gone crazy. No one falls in love over the weekend. Of course, I've tried to tell her how Zack and I spent hours and hours together. I've spent more time with him alone than I have with some guys I've dated for six months." She wrinkled her nose. "Do you think I'm being ridiculous, too?"

"No." Actually, Melody knew exactly how Leah felt.

Green eyes warming, Leah smiled. "Somehow I thought you might say that. You got to know Levi pretty well, didn't you?"

Looking at the envelope still beckoning her, Melody nodded. "We, too, became close." Because she still didn't trust herself, didn't trust her instincts when it came to men, she pushed the conversation back to her girlfriend. "So what you feel with Zack, it feels right?"

"It feels better than that. It feels amazing. Perfect."

"Perfect," Melody repeated.

"But even though my mom thinks otherwise, we're still not going to rush into anything. Zack and I both want to date for a while. Just to be sure we're in love."

"But you are?"

Leah nodded. "Absolutely. Zack makes me so happy. It's like he's been waiting for me. Like I'd been waiting for him." Leah spread out her arms. "It feels like all of a sudden, I'm part of something greater than myself. Almost like when I became a Christian."

"Truly?" With all her heart, Melody wanted to believe that such a thing was possible.

"When I found Jesus, I discovered that it had been like I was living in a tunnel, desperately only wanting to see what was in front of me, scared to look right or left, for fear that I may not like what I see . . . or like it too much. When I became a Christian, my blinders fell off. I could see the world with a better perspective. All the good and all the bad."

"Because you knew you were looking at everything through the strength of God."

"Exactly." She laughed. "Now, I'm not trying to say Zack is a saint or anything, but what he has done for me is given me that same incredible sense of belonging. I feel better, just knowing that someone cares about me. Someone loves me so much that he wants to spend the rest of his life with me."

Melody felt that way about Levi. "You're not worried his mind will change?"

"No. Because there's no little worried flutters in my

belly, warning me to be smarter. To rethink things. Plus, Zack feels the same way."

"I hope your mother will like him."

"She will," Leah said with her usual confidence. "She has to. He's going to be part of my life forever. Now, tell me about Faith, here."

Melody laughed as her daughter's eyes popped open and looked around. "She's wonderful-*gut*. Would you care to hold her?"

"Melody, I thought you'd never ask."

Chapter 29

January 6, 3:00 P.M.

Somehow, their letter writing brought them together in a way that Levi imagined nothing else ever could. For Levi, writing letters to Melody meant he could take his time to phrase his thoughts. If he messed up, he could throw away the paper and start over.

He had done that more than a few times.

But the best thing for him had been that each note he'd sent to her described his true feelings. Not ones he wished he had. Or emotions he was fumbling with, trying so hard to describe. In a strange way, he liked the exercise very much.

Melody wrote him back with regularity as well. In contrast to his painfully neat efforts, Melody's were thoughtful and deep. She wrote lots and lots . . . letting him see into the depths of her soul. Letting him see into her heart. She spared nothing in her letters, and the pages looked like it. Words were crossed out, rewritten. Then rewritten again.

And she wrote like she talked to him, he thought. Most times, she never wrote a letter in one sitting. No, she'd write a few paragraphs, then let him know that it was time to nurse Faith. Or that she was needed to help with the laundry.

Or she was taking a nap. Or, like in her last letter, she was going to go to work for a few hours while her mother watched the newborn.

And though he had no claim on Melody, hearing that she had to juggle so many things made him wish he could protect her. Watch over her, tell everyone to leave her be. At times, he'd even been tempted to send Melody some money, hating to think she was carrying not only the emotional but the financial burdens on her own as well.

But of course he did not.

However, when she very sweetly asked if he still intended to visit, he made plans to go to Kentucky within the next week.

He'd worried about taking off another day, and had uneasily shifted his weight from side to side when he'd asked Kevin if he could get off work early on Friday.

But instead of giving him grief, the other man had leaned forward with a smile. "What are your plans?"

"I'm going to go south. To Kentucky."

"To see the woman you met."

He'd been unable to keep all his secrets from his boss. "Yes," he admitted. "I need to see her."

"How are you going to get there?"

"I've hired a driver for both ways."

Kevin's brows rose. "That gets expensive, doesn't it?"

"It does, but it's worth it. I don't want to rely on bus schedules this time."

Pausing, Kevin said, "How much do you think you'll have to pay?"

Levi told him, though he wasn't comfortable about doing so. However, there was a trust between the two of them that couldn't be denied, even if at the heart of things, their relationship was still employer and employee.

"My son is twenty-two and is in need of some extra money. He's saving for an engagement ring. How would you feel if he took you both ways for half of that?"

"I'd feel happy to accept."

"Great. I'll double-check with Todd, but it shouldn't be a problem. Can he pick you up at noon from here?"

"I'll be obliged."

The trip had been easy. Todd was a likable fellow, and a careful driver. He also seemed to know that it was okay for them to not talk the whole time.

Levi was grateful for that, because the closer they came to Melody's hometown, the more nervous he became. What if she no longer was interested in him?

What if, once they saw each other again, the spark that had held him so dearly faded? Then what would happen?

As the doubts tumbled in his head and Todd exited the freeway, then made his way through the side streets, Levi once again closed his eyes and said a small, silent prayer.

Thank you, Lord, he silently prayed, *for letting me follow your will. Your path. With you I'm not as afraid. With you I know I'm never alone. And for that, I am grateful.*

"This is the address, Mr. Bender," Todd said.

Levi looked at the plain clapboard house that Todd had pulled up in front of. The yard was well kept, and he supposed it looked welcoming. "Would you mind waiting here for a bit? Melody said she'd be looking for me, but the house looks a little dark. If she's not here, I'm not quite sure what to do."

"No problem."

Levi hesitated. The original plan was for Todd to drop him off, then go check into a hotel. "You sure?"

Todd held up his phone. "I can do email from anywhere. Take your time."

Not wanting to look foolish, Levi walked quickly up the sidewalk, schooling his features to stay neutral. He knocked on the door.

After what felt like an eternity, a woman opened it a few inches and looked at him curiously. *"Jah?"*

"I'm looking for Melody Gingerich. Is this her home?"

"Who's asking?"

"I'm Levi Bender. Are you her mother?"

"I am." She looked him over, not unkindly but with true interest. Her voice softened slightly. "Melody said that you might be comin' this way."

Might? "I wrote her that I was for sure coming down." Tired of standing on her doorstep, he tilted his head in an effort to peek behind her. "Is Melody here?"

"She is not."

The statement felt like a fierce blow to his midsection. "Do you know when she'll return?"

She opened the door wider. After looking him over one more time, her distrustful expression lightened. "She's working at her coffee shop. Why don't you go over there to see her?"

"It would be all right?"

Finally smiling, Mrs. Gingerich said, "I think she'd like your visit very much." She peeked around him. "Do you have a driver?"

"He's there in that SUV."

"All right. Wait here for a moment and I'll write down the name of the restaurant and the street."

Just a few minutes later, he and Todd were back on their way. Levi hoped it wasn't a fool's errand.

As they walked into the shop, Levi turned to Todd. "How about a cup of coffee? I'll be glad to buy you one."

"I'll take you up on that. Thanks."

Levi was glad for the *Englischer*'s company. It felt awkward enough entering Great Grinds. Things would seem even stranger if he was wandering around by himself.

"May I help you?" a voice called out from behind the counter.

It took Levi a moment to realize that it was Melody's

voice; her back was to him and she was putting scones on a tray.

He'd found her.

Now, with a sense of purpose, he marched up to the counter, Todd's lanky gait following behind. "We'll take two coffees, please."

"Sure. Just a moment—Oh! Levi!"

He smiled broadly. "I told you I'd come. This here is Todd."

"Nice to meet you." A wealth of emotions rushed through her face. Surprise . . . happiness . . . worry? Warily, her gaze darted from one man to the other. Levi could swear he could see the wheels turning in her head. "So, two coffees?"

"Make mine extra large, if you can," Todd said.

"And yours, Levi?"

"Any size is fine for me."

Her lips twitched as she poured out two mugs, both very large. Levi reached in a pocket to pay, but she shook her head. "It's my treat. Would you like a scone, too? I made them fresh this morning."

Todd grinned. "Sure."

After she handed him a blueberry scone, Todd left them and went to a back table, leaving Levi to stand awkwardly at the counter. Staring. He couldn't believe he was close to her again! "I went to your home. Your mother told me you were here."

"I've been trying to put in a few hours here and there."

"And Faith? How is she?"

The first easy smile he'd seen crossed her face. "She's wonderful. Oh, Levi, I am so glad to see you. I wasn't sure if you would be able to get away."

"I couldn't think of anything I'd rather do, if you want to know the truth." He was getting tired of standing across from her. "Can you sit down for a few moments?"

"Of course. It's been quiet here."

As she walked around the counter, Levi couldn't look away. She looked as pretty as ever. Just as petite. But there was something different about Melody now.

He carried his plate and mug and followed her to a table. In the café, only two other tables were occupied. Todd was in one, and in the other, a teenage girl with headphones in her ears, was reading a book. Essentially, they were alone.

She brushed off her apron. "Do I have a stain on my dress?"

"No."

"Oh. Well, you keep looking at me. I wondered if maybe something was wrong . . ."

"There's nothing wrong. No, I mean, you look pretty." He felt his cheeks burn as she blushed. Oh, but he wished he wasn't so awkward. "You look different, too."

"I do?" She wrinkled her nose. "Different, how?"

"I don't know. Calmer?"

"Well, I'm not nine months' pregnant or in labor now," she joked. "Anyone would be calmer, I think."

He grinned, finally feeling more at ease. "There is that. But you seem happy, too. Happier."

"I am." Her eyes shone. "You are right, Levi. These days, I find that I have a lot to be happy about."

He wanted to think that he was part of her happiness. But a part of him just wasn't sure. "Of course. Faith is a true blessing."

Melody's eyes turned dreamy. "Oh, she is. Beautiful and sweet tempered."

"She would make any person's life full of joy," he agreed. And tried to think that that was enough. They had plenty of time for her to grow to love him. Plenty of time for Melody to trust him . . .

She rested her elbows on the table. "Faith does make me happy, but it is you, Levi, who've brought me back to life. When I arrived at the Brennemans', I was desperate. Desperate for family. For a sense of belonging. Desperate to have a reason to live. And then I met you."

As his body sighed in relief, he couldn't help but smile. "And I didn't give you much help in those areas at first, did I? I couldn't have been ruder to you."

"I soon learned your reasons. Levi, in so many ways, you made me find joy again."

"I feel the same way about you. I went home. I went back to work. But nothing felt right without you."

"I know. Because we wrote each other."

"And wrote. But the letters weren't enough. I couldn't stay away."

"I'm so glad you are here. How long will you stay?"

"Well, here's the thing . . . I plan to stay here long enough to convince you to marry me."

Her eyes widened. "Marry?"

"I know we haven't known each other long," he said quickly. "I know we should wait. We should be patient.

Write more letters . . . but Melody, I already know you have my heart."

Eyes wide, she stared at him.

Levi's mouth went dry. Oh, why had he been so impatient? He was doing this all wrong. He should have waited longer. Perhaps another month? Maybe two?

"Yes," she said.

"Yes?" Levi reached for her hands. "That's it?"

Her beautiful golden brown eyes shone. Gave him hope. "Isn't that enough?"

"It is more than enough," he whispered. "I love you, Melody. I love you more than you will ever know."

She leaned closer. "That's where you're wrong, Levi Bender. I do already know. Because I feel the very same way."

Tenderly, he kissed her. Right there, in the back of the coffee shop.

Right there, on the twelfth day after Christmas. On one of the most glorious days of the year.

Dear Reader:

A year or two before I got married, I spent the majority of Christmas Day in a hotel room. Oh, it was a very nice hotel room. The bed was comfortable. There was room service, a big bathtub with lots of bubble bath and lotion . . . a television with lots of channels. But, well, it wasn't where I wanted to be.

I tried my hardest to make the best of things. I ordered room service. I pretended I was glad I wasn't in a noisy house with lots of people and too many dishes. But I wasn't.

Actually, as the hours wore on, I became pretty depressed. I had a view of the front parking lot, and it looked to me that everyone else in the world was traveling in groups, each person holding more packages than the last. Everyone looked happy. Exuberant. I was not.

Every Christmas since, things have been different. Never again have I spent the day alone. Instead, I've been surrounded by family and friends. Sometimes the day is so busy, with cooking and cleaning and visiting and wrapping that

I've even yearned for a moment or two of peace! Maybe some of you have felt the same way.

Now I have to think that God had plans for me way back then—when I spent the day looking out the window. Perhaps he was giving me the tools to write a novel about two lonely visitors who seek refuge in an inn for Christmas.

Being able to write this story has truly been a gift for me. I loved writing a story about two people finding hope and joy and God's grace on Christmas Day. And, of course, I was happy to return to the characters in the Sisters of the Heart series.

So this Christmas, I hope you have joy. And peace. And the knowledge that even if you happen to be sitting by yourself in a hotel room, you are never truly alone.

God Bless, and Merry Christmas!

Shelley Shepard Gray

P.S. I love to hear from readers. Please visit my Web site, www.shelleyshepardgray.com, "friend" me on Facebook, or write to me at:

Shelley Shepard Gray
10663 Loveland-Madeira Rd. #167
Loveland, OH 45140

Questions for Discussion

1. At first, Katie Lundy resents the arrival of Melody and Levi because she feels they've ruined her family's holiday. What is your idea of the "perfect" Christmas? Do you recall a Christmas when things didn't go as planned?

2. Both Levi and Melody sought to escape their problems by spending Christmas at the Brenneman Bed and Breakfast. Ironically, instead of avoiding their worries, they were able to finally heal. Has "taking a break" from your problems ever helped you?

3. Melody never wavered in her decision to keep her baby. Was this the right choice? Would you have blamed her if she had wanted to give it up for adoption?

4. Levi feels his pride is to blame for his wife and baby's death. Is this the case? Has your pride ever pushed you to make a poor decision?

5. Mrs. Brenneman makes the choice to include her guests in family activities. Levi goes hunting with the men and Melody joins the women in the kitchen. How did including Levi and Melody help their old wounds heal?

6. Leah was determined to do whatever it took to be by Melody's side on Christmas Day. Have you ever gone out of your way for a special friend? What were the results of your efforts?

7. Leah and Zack's romance was fairly sweet and straightforward compared to Melody and Levi's. Is falling in love ever like that? Leah says she knows Zack is the "right" man for her. Do you think their relationship will last?

8. The Amish rarely decorate for Christmas. There is no tree, no nativity set, nor a wreath on the door. No Christmas carols are sung. However, many do exchange Christmas cards, bake Christmas cookies, and sometimes exchange one or two simple, meaningful gifts. How do these traditions compare to the way your family celebrates the holiday?

9. It is a tradition in the Brenneman family to read the story of Jesus's birth from the book of Luke. What are some of your traditions?

10. The concept of Grace is an integral one to the story. How do you define "Grace"? Can you think of a time in your life when you've felt blessed by it?

Recipes from GRACE

(*From* Our Family's Favorite Recipes)

MOLASSES COOKIES

1 cup butter
1 cup sugar
2 eggs
1 cup molasses
1 cup sour milk
4 cups flour
2 teaspoons ginger
1 teaspoon cinnamon
½ teaspoon salt
2 teaspoons baking soda

Cream together butter, sugar, eggs, molasses, and 1 teaspoon baking soda. Add dry ingredients with remaining 1 teaspoon baking soda in sour milk. Bake at 375 degrees.

BEST CINNAMON ROLLS

2 packets yeast
2 ½ cups water
1 box yellow cake mix
3 eggs
⅓ cup oil
6 cups flour
1 teaspoon salt

Melt margarine, brown sugar, and cinnamon mix just enough to coat the tops of rolls.

Dissolve yeast in warm water. Add cake mix, eggs, oil, 1 cup flour, and salt. Beat until bubbles appear. Slowly, add remaining flour or enough to make soft dough that you can knead. Let rise until double.

Roll dough ¼ inch, spread with margarine, sugar, and cinnamon mix. Roll up, and slice. Place slices in greased pans and let rise until double. Bake at 350 degrees, 20 to 30 minutes. Top with powdered sugar to glaze when cool. Very good!

ORANGE SLUSH
(This is delicious for breakfast.)

3 cups water
2 cups sugar

Boil for five minutes. Let cool.

Add:
1 6-ounce can frozen orange juice
1 large can crushed pineapple (do not drain)
8 mashed bananas

Mix and freeze to a slush consistency.

BREAKFAST CASSEROLE

6 eggs
Ham, sausage, or fried bacon
Onion, salt, and pepper to taste
2 cups milk
6 pieces old bread
Velveeta slices

Beat the six eggs. Add breakfast meat and seasonings. Pour into greased cake pan. Leave in refrigerator overnight. In the morning, heat oven to 350 degrees. Put Velveeta slices on top. Bake half an hour.

ORANGE CRANBERRY BREAD

½ cup butter
¾ cup sugar
1 egg
1 teaspoon grated orange peel
⅓ cup chopped pecans
¾ cup coarsely chopped cranberries
2 ½ cups flour
2 teaspoons baking powder
½ teaspoon salt
⅓ cup milk
⅔ cup orange juice

Glaze:
1 cup powdered sugar
4 teaspoons orange juice

Heat oven to 350 degrees. Combine butter, sugar, egg, and orange peel. Add juice, milk, and dry ingredients. Add nuts and cranberries last.

Spoon into greased loaf pan. Bake 50 to 60 minutes. Mix powdered sugar and orange for glaze, spread over cooled bread.

Stay Tuned for
Shelley Shepard Gray's
Next Novel

The Caregiver

Coming soon from

AVON
INSPIRE

Spring 2011

Monday, June 7, 11:59 P.M.
South Bend, Indiana

"So . . . it looks like I'm your seatmate."

Slowly Lucy Troyer opened her eyes and turned to the deep-sounding voice. Then couldn't help but stare. The man speaking to her was Amish. And, she just realized, he'd spoken to her in Pennsylvania Dutch.

She blinked. How could that be? From the time she'd left the train station in Kalamazoo, she'd hardly come across more than a handful of people like herself, and they'd been in the train station in Chicago.

As her eyes continued to focus, the man—who really was too handsome for his own good—had the nerve to wink. "I know, it's enough to make ya smile, ain't it?" he asked, bright blue eyes shining underneath the soggy brim of his black felt hat. "The coach attendant took me through practically this whole train here, and I didn't spy a single other Plain traveler. Until you. And now . . . here we are."

Yes, here they were, she repeated to herself, slowly wondering if she'd ever seen another jaw so fine. Or shoulders so broad . . .

When she noticed he was still standing, and she was still staring, Lucy shook herself out of her reverie. "I'm sorry. Am I taking up both the seats?"

"Not so much. But it would be to your benefit to scoot over as much as you can, if you don't mind. I'm near soaked to the skin." Shrugging off his wet jacket, he grinned broadly. "You're right lucky you were inside this train instead of waiting in the weather. The storm is a terrible one, for sure."

"I fell asleep more than an hour ago. I didn't even realize it was raining." She scooted over a bit and pushed her skirts more neatly around her. "There. I hope this is better?"

"You're fine. Of course, you're fine," he murmured as he pulled a modern-looking backpack up from the floor and hefted it into the chrome container above their heads.

Then, with the pleased expression of completing a task, he joined her, bringing with him the scent of rain and man and something so fresh it made her think of spring.

Despite their best intentions, his pants brushed against her dress, making the once terribly roomy pair of seats seem suddenly narrow and confining.

Around them, in the dim light of the overhead fluorescents, the other passengers mumbled and snored. After a faint call of 'all aboard,' the train chugged into motion.

As the station slowly faded from view, her new seatmate

spoke. "I haveta admit, I don't fancy boarding a train at midnight. But what do ya do, huh? We're bound by the train schedule."

"Indeed." Lucy ached to think of something else to say, something far more significant, but her mind went blank.

But instead of looking at her strangely, her one-word answer seemed to amuse him. "So, I'm guessing you didn't board here in South Bend. When did you get on?"

"Back in Kalamazoo, Michigan."

"So you've been traveling for some time."

"*Jah.* Hours and hours. I boarded a different train back in Kalamazoo, then got on this one in Chicago."

"You've had quite an exciting day, then."

Again, she noticed that his whole demeanor was patient. Kind. Not searching for faults.

With effort, she pushed back the hint of unease she felt rushing forward, heating her cheeks. *Just because a handsome man looks like Paul, it doesn't mean he's like him inside,* she cautioned herself.

Feeling his stare, Lucy knew he was still waiting for her to say something. "You could say that my day's been exciting," she said slowly. "At least, it has been for me. It's my first train trip by myself."

"We'll have to stick together then, *jah?*"

Lucy turned her head away so he wouldn't see the surprise in her eyes. This man was quickly turning her stomach into knots. She wasn't used to talking to men she didn't know. Especially one on one.

Obviously misjudging her uneasiness, he cleared his throat. "Have I apologized to you for waking you up?"

"There's no need for that. If I was sleeping, it wasn't too deeply. Just dozing."

He leaned back on his chair and wiggled a bit as it creaked and groaned. "A doze is probably all we'll get. This train's sure seen better days, ain't so?"

"I think so," she said softly. But of course, she'd seen better days, as well. It used to be, talking with a man would make her smile. Now she was on edge.

Waiting for him to say something disparaging. The way her husband used to.

Next to her, the man fidgeted again, finally pulling out a newspaper that she hadn't even noticed he'd slipped in the pocket of the seat in front of them. "By the way, I'm Calvin."

"I'm Lucy."

Calvin inclined his head. "Lucy, I'm pleased to meet you."

"Uh. Yes," she said, then feeling like a fool again, she turned toward the window and closed her eyes. But though she tried her best to relax, she was finding it next to impossible. She was too aware of his presence. His smile. His easy way of moving.

And the horrible knowledge that once again she was noticing a too-handsome man she really knew nothing about.

Just like she'd done with Paul.

As Lucy closed her eyes next to him, Calvin shook his head with regret. When he'd first saw the woman next to him, he'd been thanking his lucky stars. She was a pretty thing, and looked so pleasant. Lucy's hair was the color of dark golden honey, and her light golden eyes looked like a clear sky on an early winter morning.

But her attitude had been so skittish—almost as if she'd wished he would sit next to anyone but her.

Almost as if she'd been afraid of him.

He frowned. Never before in his twenty-six years had a girl looked at him with such apprehension. On the contrary, most seemed to go out of their way to be good company.

He'd always taken that for granted, he supposed. It was what came of being Calvin Weaver, the oldest son of the Weaver family—the biggest landowners in Jacob's Crossing.

As he turned the page of *The Budget*, and tried to fold the paper so it wouldn't brush against Lucy's dress, he glanced her way again.

Besides her golden hair and matching eyes, she was altogether lovely. Slim and blessed with full cheeks. With some surprise, Calvin realized she was older than he'd first thought, too. Most likely she was closer to his age than not.

Surely she wasn't some shy young girl.

And she also didn't seem to actually be sleeping—more like she was just pretending to sleep. Obviously so she wouldn't have to talk to him.

So what was it that had set her off? Had he said something that could be misconstrued? Replaying their brief conversation in his mind, he could think of nothing untoward.

Well, perhaps she was simply a reserved sort of person. Bored with the paper, Calvin looked around the rest of the train car. Perhaps he'd find a congenial man to visit with? But the dozen or so people who shared the space with him all looked to be happily occupied or fast asleep.

Almost against his will, he pulled the worn letter out from his jacket's inside pocket. In the relative privacy of his seat, he smoothed out the creases, rubbing his thumb against the folds. Over the words he had memorized six weeks ago, but couldn't seem to let go of.

His last letter from Gwen.

There was no reason for him to still have the note. He knew why Gwen had broken up with him. She'd fallen in love with someone else. One of his friends.

Everyone expected Gwen and Abraham to declare themselves any day.

And that knowledge—and their betrayal—hurt more terribly than he'd imagined it could.

Dear Calvin, the letter began. *I fear I must finally be honest with you . . .*

She'd feared. Finally. Each phrase hurt him anew. Calvin blinked, then, like an addict, focused on the words again, further down the page.

Abraham and I, we can't help our feelings, you see . . .

As the words swam in front of him, a conversation with his brothers floated forward.

"Why don't you go to Indiana for a spell," his youngest brother Graham had told him. "There's no need for you to witness their courting."

But running away had seemed weak, and he'd told them that.

His brother Loyal had simply laughed. "What does it matter if people think you're weak or strong? All that matters is how you feel. And for the record, I think you have every right to feel betrayed."

"*Jah*," Graham added. "They went and fell in love right under your nose. Get away from here for a week or so. Clear your head."

Well, Graham never had been one to mince words.

But though his brothers' advice made perfect sense . . . and though his mother had wholeheartedly supported his vacation, Calvin had hemmed and hawed. He'd stayed up long nights and prayed for answers. For the right answers. But the only advice that rang true to him were the words from his brothers.

That there was no shame in being hurt.

So, he'd left Jacob's Crossing and journeyed west to Indianapolis. He'd visited his Uncle James, who'd become an *Englischer* before Calvin had been born. His uncle hadn't asked about his reason for being there. Perhaps he'd already heard. But instead of treating him to questions, Uncle James had driven him around his hometown.

Together, they'd visited museums, and the racetrack. They'd walked city blocks and ridden bicycles. Slowly, Calvin began to feel less depressed about his reasons for being there and had begun to take comfort in the blessings he was given. He admired the tall buildings and the intricately designed gardens. He bought a dozen postcards to show his brothers.

Afterward, so he could justify his week of rest, he traveled north and went to a horse auction.

And then boarded this train.

In mere hours, he'd be back to Jacob's Crossing. Back to where everything was familiar and almost comfortable.

If he tried real hard, Calvin was sure he'd be able to

tell everyone that Gwen and Abraham's new affection for each other hardly mattered to him at all. Even though he was now the one lying.

He knew he needed to throw out Gwen's note and move on, in mind as well as deed.

But as if his hands were of their own accord, he neatly folded the paper back again and slipped it into his pocket. There would be another time. Another, better time.

Just like there would be time to move forward, and finally take out Edith. Like his heartbreak, it had been no secret that she was wearing her heart on her sleeve for him. Edith would make a wonderful wife.

And though he doubted he would ever love her, Calvin was beginning to think that love was an overvalued thing anyway. All it really ever did was make a man make a fool of himself.

And who needed that?

He turned back to the *Budget* when a child two rows back whined. The noise startled a babe. Its cries encouraged several children to raise their voices to be heard. And still Lucy pretended to sleep beside him.

If he hadn't been so well-mannered, Calvin would have snorted. Between the baby crying, the *kinner* yelling, the rain pounding overhead, and the muggy, almost too-warm air surrounding them, sleep was near impossible.

At last Lucy opened her eyes. "Perhaps trying to sleep was a foolish idea."

Calvin waited a few seconds, flipped the page, and then answered. "Not so foolish, I don't think. But perhaps one doomed for failure."

"We must be heading into the storm," she said. "I just heard thunder."

"*Jah*. Things do seem to be getting a worse, don't they?"

She scooted to the edge of her seat. "Would you mind if I got a project out of my bag? I might as well crochet."

He stood up. "I'll pull your bag down for you."

"I can do it—"

"*Jah*, but it is easier for me. I'm right here." He'd just reached his arms up to grab hold of the fabric handle when the train rocked again.

"Oh!" Lucy said.

Outside, a flash of lightning illuminated the sky. Inside, the row of florescent lights flickered. The train rocked again.

Almost losing his balance, Calvin reached for the chrome bar and gripped it hard.

"*Gebb acht*!" Lucy warned.

"I *am* being careful. Don't worry," he murmured. Just as the lights flickered again, then seemed to give up the fight. Shrouding them in darkness.

Beside him, Lucy cried out.

Mary Lou Zinsser

Shelley Shepard Gray

SHELLEY SHEPARD GRAY is the beloved author of the Sisters of the Heart series, including *Hidden*, *Wanted*, and *Forgiven*. Before writing, she was a teacher in both Texas and Colorado. She now writes full time and lives in southern Ohio with her husband and two children. When not writing, Shelley volunteers at church, reads, and enjoys walking her miniature dachshund on her town's scenic bike trail.